KING TAKES QUEEN

Ladies of Risk, Book 3

Rachel Ann Smith

ARE YOU SIGNED UP FOR DRAGONBLADE'S BLOG?

You'll get the latest news and information on exclusive giveaways, exclusive excerpts, coming releases, sales, free books, cover reveals and more.

Check out our complete list of authors, too!

No spam, no junk. That's a promise!

Sign Up Here

www.dragonbladepublishing.com

Dearest Reader;

Thank you for your support of a small press. At Dragonblade Publishing, we strive to bring you the highest quality Historical Romance from some of the best authors in the business. Without your support, there is no 'us', so we sincerely hope you adore these stories and find some new favorite authors along the way.

Happy Reading!

CEO, Dragonblade Publishing

**Additional Dragonblade books by
Author Rachel Ann Smith**

Ladies of Risk Series
An Earl Unmasked (Book 1)
The Duke of Aces (Book 2)
King Takes Queen (Book 3)
A Yuletide Wedding (Novella)

CHAPTER ONE

S EATED BEHIND HIS desk, Anthony MacMillian, Earl of Drake, stared down at his most prized possession, which sat in the middle of his palm. A stone that he carried about always. It wasn't a precious gemstone of any sort. No, the round, slightly translucent pebble had been plucked from the garden. Selected by none other than Lady Minerva Malbury, the woman he'd been in love with for longer than he could remember. Anthony's lips curved as he relived the moment from years ago, when Minerva had used the stone to place him in check, during their one and only chess game. He'd never considered losing an option prior to that day, but he'd forfeited to Minerva for the simple fact that he knew it would make her happy. And it was worth every ounce of his pride to see the girl that had claimed his heart smile at him as if he had bestowed upon her her greatest wish. Minerva was unlike any other. She was a brilliant strategist, a devoted sister, and the most alluring female of his acquaintance.

Anthony's head snapped to the left to face the window of his private study. The wooden frame rattled, and a shiny black Heisman appeared before the rest of Benedict Malbury, the honorable Viscount of Kent, materialized. Kent, his best friend, and Minerva's eldest brother, had finally decided to make an appearance this eve. Anthony hated remaining idle, but he'd had no choice but to wait for the newlywed Lord Kent to answer his plea for an audience.

Slightly bent at the waist, Anthony slowly returned his blade to his boot. Kent was no threat, or at least he wasn't at the moment.

Feet firmly planted on the floor, Kent sealed the window back into place and straightened to his full height before he firmly tugged on his coat sleeves and turned to face Anthony. "This had best be a matter of dire straits, as you portrayed it to be in your missive, or you'll owe me a crate of brandy for summoning me from my bed and wife."

Did Kent suspect his motives? Anthony pocketed the stone and steepled his fingers. "I'm leaving England for an undefined period, and I need your assistance."

Kent strode over to the fire and removed his gloves. Palms held out toward the flames, he asked, "You're leaving? The first session of Parliament is in two days. You can't leave now." He rubbed his hands together and turned. "You can't simply leave Town now."

Anthony shrugged his shoulders. It wasn't his choice.

Kent stripped out of his greatcoat, sat in the wing-back chair opposite Anthony, and arched a brow.

"You know I hate sailing." Anthony masked the shudder of fear that rolled down his spine. He'd heard too many tales of lives lost at sea. The seas were dangerous and unpredictable. And boats, boats were fragile and unreliable. He was a land-faring man, preferring the earth beneath his feet, safe and solid.

"My wife is abed and waiting. Get to the point."

"The Head of the Foreign Office has issued an ultimatum— I'm to board the *Quarter Moon* at first light…or challenge Minerva to a chess match." He mumbled the second half of his statement, hoping Kent would ignore it, and held his breath.

Kent leaned forward, one arm on his knee supporting his weight. "I thought you declined the offer to join the department years ago."

Anthony sighed. Thank goodness his friend had overlooked

the mention of his sister. "Indeed, I have. Repeatedly, however, the Head of the Foreign Office made it clear it is no longer an offer but a directive."

"Interesting. Where do they intend to send you?"

"To hell, as far as I'm concerned," he replied.

Minerva was planning to head west to America, and they were sending him in the opposite direction, to the east—India.

Kent glared at him, lips thinned and brows knitted. The intimidating action worked to gain the truth from the man's siblings, but it wouldn't work on Anthony. He could easily evade the question with a series of short, redirecting statements, but he wasn't in the mood for riddles.

"India. They are shipping me off to India, but I'm not ready to leave, not until I know—"

"You know what?"

Anthony raised his gaze to meet Kent's questioning features. It was time. Time to stop pretending he didn't care. "I can't leave until I know Minerva is safe and happily wed."

Kent jumped up from his seat. "Safe! You promised to keep Mansville and his lot away from her until I arrived."

With his best friend looming over him, Anthony answered, "Besides a very brief encounter at the races at Fulham, Mansville hasn't been within one hundred yards of Minerva." He didn't bother to add that he suspected that the interfering, meddling, but well-meaning Head of the Foreign Office more than likely had played a hand in ensuring Minerva wasn't bothered by her arch-nemesis. In this instance, he wished he was wrong, but he rarely made errors about these matters.

Kent settled a hand on his right hip and shook his head. "Please don't tell me you dragged me out of my bed to ask me to look over my own damn sister."

"You are like a brother to me, and—"

"I know...and Minerva is like a sister."

His friend's pompous, all-knowing demeanor grated on Anthony's nerves. He replied, "No. Not like a sister. That's what I've been meaning to tell you… For years I haven't—"

Kent raised his hand. "Stop. You need say no more. I'm not a total idiot. I've gleaned over the past year that you've had more than brotherly feelings for Minerva. What I don't understand is if that is how you truly felt, why, for the past two Seasons, have you failed to step up and challenge her to a game of chess? Why allow Mansville and his cronies the opportunity to win her hand?"

There were a multitude of reasons in Anthony's mind as to why he couldn't marry Minerva, but which would appease Kent's curiosity? He stood, so he was on equal footing with Kent. "Would you have given me your blessing to challenge her?"

Kent didn't immediately answer. Instead, the man normally so sure of himself shrugged. "You're my oldest and closest friend. I know everything there is to know about you."

A pang of guilt hit Anthony square in the chest. The truth was that Kent didn't really know all there was to know about Anthony, only details of his life that Anthony had carefully decided to share. "Then you would agree…I'm not the right gentleman for Minerva. She deserves someone who can fulfill her every dream. Her every wish. A gentleman who would make her life fuller."

Kent's shoulders stiffened. "No. In fact, I was going to say, while I have excellent recall, dating back to the day I first met you at Eton, I don't know much about your past. You never speak of your deceased parents. You never talk of any family relations; you treat your staff like family and not like hired help. I love you like a brother, yet I sometimes feel like I don't really know you, and that is what worries me. It is what prevents me from encouraging you to challenge Minerva."

"I've never hidden the truth from you." It wasn't a lie. Anthony merely avoided certain topics.

He walked over to the sideboard. If he was going to discuss his past, he needed a drink. He splashed brandy into two tumblers. Anthony downed one quickly before refilling his glass, then returned to hand Kent his. "You could have simply asked, and I would have told you."

"Well then…I'm asking now, what were you like prior to us meeting? What of your family? I want to know it all." Kent, mercifully, glanced down at the beverage in his hand and swirled the amber liquid around and around.

There was no good reason to not answer Kent's questions directly, except if Anthony's reply wasn't carefully crafted, Kent would be privy to the source of all his insecurities.

He inhaled and began. "Very well. My mother died during childbirth, not a unique tragedy, and my father went to his maker when I was five. My uncle Liam became my guardian, and it was he who raised me until he shipped me off to school, and a year later, he too left this earth. At that time, I inherited the title Earl of Drake and simultaneously became Laird MacMillian."

Anthony left out the detail that his mother had been the third wife that his father had sent to the grave, trying to provide him with an heir. MacMillians were a determined and loyal lot, though not the most fertile. Even Uncle Liam had given up on ever siring a son. Anthony's cousins, all female, were older than him by many years and were already married by the time he was even born. He swore he would remain a bachelor, for he would not knowingly kill his wife in the vain attempt to carry on a title that was no more than a burden.

Kent raised his gaze to meet his and blinked twice. "A laird?"

"Aye. I've clansmen and land that borders Avondale's estate to the north, in Scotland. Avondale and I have not always seen eye to eye as neighbors."

"That explains why Avondale denied you an invitation to his house party, and why you were still able to report on my sister's activities." Kent drained the last of his drink, reached out to take Anthony's empty glass, and strode to the sideboard.

"Exactly. But I've not asked you here tonight to talk about Isadora or your future brother-in-law Avondale." His annoying neighbor's name left a bitter taste on Anthony's tongue.

"Then why have you asked me to come?" Kent returned

empty-handed and remained standing, devoid of any sign of his prior self. Prior to marriage, the man would have overfilled the tumblers and made himself comfortable in one of the wing-back chairs, intending to stay until the first rays of sun rose over the horizon. Yes, Kent was a changed man, and that was what Anthony was counting on.

"I need you to talk some sense into Minerva. She has plans to leave, to venture to America in a month."

"In a month, you say." Kent's brow creased. "I was not aware she and Aunt Adelaide had planned to leave so soon."

"You knew she was to venture abroad?" Impossible! Why would Kent permit such a thing? Ugh. Minerva and her mind tricks. Her ability to convince others to yield to her plans was damn annoying.

"Of course. We Malbury siblings don't keep secrets from one another. She has tickets to board the *Quarter Moon*," Kent boasted.

"And you fully support her venturing across the pond? Wait…did you say the *Quarter Moon*?"

"I did. I spoke to the captain myself. Captain Bane assured me the journey was perfectly safe, one he'd completed many a time."

"Bloody hell! It takes six months to reach either location—"

Kent interrupted, "And?"

"And…either Minerva's plans are a farce, or I'm not being sent to India… We can't both be boarding the *Quarter Moon*."

"Why are you so surprised? You know my sister Minerva always has several plays in action. No one really knows which is her real plan." Kent shrugged into his coat. "My thanks for trying to warn me of my sister's wayward plan, but now that the whole family is in London, we shall ensure Minerva is happily wed before she can even consider executing whatever devilish plan she may have."

Kent opened the window and crawled out. They were no longer young bucks sneaking about Town, yet Anthony appreciated the nod to the times when they were both reckless and carefree. To be fair, Kent was the reckless one, while he was considered carefree. How quickly things could change over a summer.

Anthony slumped into the chair in front of the fire. He should have noted the inconsistency in information. He was typically four steps ahead of most, but when it came to Minerva, he became a total dunderhead.

CHAPTER TWO

N O MATTER HOW long she stared at the window, it wouldn't make the man she longed to see appear. Minerva punched her pillow twice and then laid her head back down. Except, her eyes refused to close. The drapes fluttered. A dark figure emerged from the heavy velvet material that would block out the daylight in a few hours. Who dared to enter her rooms in the middle of the night? It wasn't Anthony, for the skin on the back of her neck didn't prickle and her heartbeat remained steady.

Minerva slid her hand around her pistol under her pillow. "Halt, or you won't see the morn."

"Phyllis will not be happy with you if you shoot me dead."

Blasted brothers. "Benedict!" Minerva jumped out of bed and launched herself at the dark figure. She wrapped her arms tight around her brother, whom she hadn't seen in months. It wasn't the longest period that they had been apart, but her plans for the future loomed over her, pushing her to take advantage of every minute she had left with her siblings. "You know better than to sneak into my chambers." Why had her brother entered via the window and not through the house?

"I must speak to you in private. And to be clear, I wasn't sneaking about. I simply wished not to disturb the staff." Benedict gave her a quick squeeze and then released her.

She grabbed her shawl from the end of her bed and wrapped

it about her shoulders. "What is so important that you deemed it necessary to climb up the trellis at…" She glanced out the window, but with the clouds masking the moonlight, it was hard to determine the hour. "…at such an ungodly hour. Wait. Why are you not abed with Phyllis?" She studied her brother's features closely and identified concern and worry. "You haven't made a muck of your marriage already, have you?"

Benedict leaned against her bedpost. "Your lack of confidence in me wounds me deeply."

"You can't fault me. You've not had a great example for the role of husband." Fact was her parents were a poor example all round, both far too self-absorbed to care for anyone but themselves.

Benedict sighed. "You have matters to worry about other than whether or not I'm making a hash of my marriage with Phyllis."

A trickle of fear prickled the skin on the back of her neck. What had Benedict discovered? Did he know her plans for the upcoming Season? She searched her sibling's features once more. Brows knitted, and lips thinned into a line. He was worried. But for whom?

Her brother bowed his head and kneaded the muscles at the back of his neck. "Drake is in danger of being banished. Sentenced to live on foreign lands, and it will be all your fault." Benedict pinned her with an accusatory stare.

Her breath hitched. Drake was in danger. Her heart flipped in her chest, as it always did at the mention of her brother's best friend's name. The man she'd fallen in love with as a teen and who had subsequently rejected her year after year. She'd sworn to bury her feelings for the man. Decided to pursue her passion for the stage, rather than hold out hope Drake might act upon the magnetic attraction that existed between them.

Minerva crossed her arms over her chest and glared at her brother. Benedict was the family heir and five years her senior, but it was she who had managed the family for years. She wasn't about to relinquish her power simply because she was his only sister to remain unattached. "Banished? Where? By whom?"

"Drake has been ordered by the Head of the Foreign Office to board the *Quarter Moon* at first light, which is scheduled to depart for India."

Minerva swallowed the groan that bubbled up in her chest at the mention of the Head of the Foreign Office. The leader of foreign affairs was a thorn in Minerva's side. Always meddling and intervening in her schemes. "How is any of that my fault?"

The twitch of her brother's jaw muscle was a warning sign. Whatever it was he was about to impart was, in his opinion, extremely serious, and it mattered deeply to him. "The Head of the Foreign Office gave him a choice. Challenge you to a chess match or leave."

Her hands clenched into fists. The blasted challenge. She should never have listened to Drake and his idiotic idea to delay marriage.

Her mind screamed, *Liar.* Drake hadn't exactly devised the challenge or the terms. The man had simply made a passing comment. A comment that she had interpreted to mean he wanted to offer for her hand, but he was simply not ready. It had been one moment of weakness, allowing her heart to rule instead of logic. She had learned her lesson. Never allow your heart to interfere with well-devised plans. She was done waiting for Drake.

Liar.

She ignored her wayward thoughts, stiffened her spine and resolve, and replied, "Again, I fail to see how any of this is my doing." Knees weak, she stepped back to sink onto the edge of the bed. The reality of her brother's news sank in. Faced with the choice of marriage to her or banishment, Drake had chosen a life away from everything and everyone he loved.

"You can not continue to reject someone repeatedly and not suffer the consequences."

Minerva blinked and peered up at Benedict. "Whom exactly

are you referring to?"

Her brother's jaw clenched, another sign Benedict was close to losing all patience. "I'm speaking about the both of you. You *and* Drake. The two of you have repeatedly declined offers from the Head of the Foreign Office."

Bah. One would think the head of foreign affairs would have more important matters to occupy their time than devising a plan to punish either Drake or herself for their refusals.

Except if Benedict's intel was correct, Drake was to suffer the consequences for the both of them. Blast it all. She couldn't afford another diversion, not when she was amidst finalizing the details of her own scheme to explore her options for the future. Double blast. Drake shouldn't be punished for her deeds. Her decisions. Her choices.

Benedict placed a hand on her shoulder. "I apologize. The thought of my best friend residing on the other side of the world has me panicked. I shouldn't have been so harsh."

Minerva stood, dislodging her brother's touch. She was well aware that Drake was like a brother to Benedict. The two were inseparable. "No need to apologize. I understand how much Drake means to you."

"To all of us."

Benedict was right. Drake was like a brother to all the Malbury siblings—that was, with the exception of her. Brothers didn't make your heart flutter or your pulse race. But that was in the past. For the last three months, Minerva had carefully avoided the man and steeled her heart against him.

She needed to redirect the conversation back to the conundrum. "What would you have me do, Benedict? Agree to join Avondale and his lot in conducting clandestine investigations?"

"You're right. I wouldn't have supported the idea. It's too bloody dangerous for a lady."

Argh. Her brother was such a male chauvinist sometimes.

Reining in her temper, she replied, "Tell me, why do you suppose the Head of the Foreign Office would even suggest

Drake challenge me to a chess match? They must be aware of my declaration."

"I've been mulling that exact question over and over since I left Drake's dwellings." Hands behind his back, Benedict began to pace. "Mayhap the Head of the Foreign Office believes Drake could defeat you. He marries you. They convince him to join, thereby gaining both of you as assets. *Or* they wish to know which of the two of you they should continue to pursue. *Or* they simply take delight in interfering in others' lives. *Or—*"

Minerva stepped in front of her brother and asked, "Do you believe Drake could defeat me?"

"Assuming you didn't want him to?" Benedict's eyes stared back at her, clear and intent. "Yes. Yes, I believe there is still a strong possibility he could. The two of you think alike. Frighteningly so."

She shook her head. "I don't understand what you want me to do."

"I want you to play Drake."

Hands clenched at her sides, she asked, "And what of your rule that friends don't dally with a friend's sister?"

"If it's a choice of losing my best friend and not knowing of his welfare or location or losing my sister to a friend...I choose the latter."

"What?" Minerva grabbed her brother by the forearm and tugged him back to the window he'd entered. "Out!"

Halfway in and halfway out, Benedict turned and said, "If he were to somehow win, I know Drake would protect you. He would see to it that you are well taken care of."

With a shove, Minerva pushed her brother out the window. "Benedict Malbury, I love ye, but you can be a pompous prig. Now leave before I hurt you."

She didn't disagree with her brother. Drake would fulfill his husbandly duties without complaint, but she wanted more. She wished for a husband who desired her, who loved her and who wanted to spend time with her. Drake had made it clear to her—

his desire was for another. He'd given his heart to another. He even shared that he'd spent many an hour seeking out the location of a lady. A lady she knew well.

Her mind was a whirl, volleying from rage at Benedict and his misguided statements, to concern for a man that she couldn't stop loving, back to anger at herself for her inability to remain indifferent. If she didn't intervene, Drake would be sent away, and her siblings' distress would fall on her shoulders.

She rushed into her adjoining changing room and slipped out of her nightgown. Hands fumbling through drawers, Minerva mumbled, "Where are they?" She searched for her brother Gregory's old breeches and a lawn shirt that she had stashed away for such occasions.

A sigh of relief escaped her as she found Gregory's discarded clothing under a mound of silk stockings. A shiver ran down her spine as she donned the items. She would need a greatcoat, but Isadora had Gregory's castoff.

With a sigh, Minerva made her way through the house. She was exhausted, and the idea of traipsing across Town to sneak into Drake's residence caused her stomach to knot.

Minerva tiptoed down to the empty foyer, where Gregory's greatcoat was haphazardly draped over the stair railing. How peculiar. The Malbury butler was meticulous. He wasn't one to leave Gregory's garments lying about.

With no one in sight, Minerva slipped on the coat and made her way out the front door. She halted at the sight of her most trusted footman standing at the ready by the Malbury coach.

Benedict. It had to be his doing. Blasted older brothers.

Minerva's lips curved into a smile as she stepped up into the coach. Her brother knew her well. He just didn't know the truth about his best friend's infatuation for another woman. Benedict had left it up to Minerva to sort out matters, as usual. She never shied away from responsibility, and she wasn't about to start now, even if it meant placing her heart in danger once again.

CHAPTER THREE

TRUNKS PACKED, DRAKE strode across his bedchambers and leaned his forehead against the cool glass plane and closed his eyes. *All shall be fine.* Despite his having repeated the mantra over and over silently within, and out loud for the last several hours, both his heart and mind remained unconvinced. As the hours passed and the threat of being banished to foreign soil loomed—to be surrounded by strangers, without a familiar face close by for the foreseeable future—the waves of fear continued to mount and roll through him again and again.

A hand fell upon his left shoulder. He whirled about, grappling with the intruder.

How in damnation had someone entered his home, his chambers, undetected?

Soft curves pressed against his forearms and his favorite mixed scent of lemons and vanilla filled his lungs. Minerva.

Instead of releasing her like he knew he should, he inhaled deeply and nuzzled her neck. If he wasn't going to be able to see her for months, more likely years, he was going to take full advantage of the hoyden's mistake of entering his chambers alone.

"Anthony Joseph Edmund MacMillian! Release me this instant."

Oh, how he loved it when she recited his full name. It meant she was flustered. She uttered the extra syllables when she needed another moment or two to think.

He slowly eased his hold on her and reluctantly took a step back.

She spun around to face him. Her lush lips were thinned into a straight line. Dammit. Even when the woman was hopping mad at him, his blood pumped faster through his veins. Minerva's ability to put him on tilt had intensified over the years. A mere glance from her had him questioning his every thought, every decision, every acute physical response to her presence. And as each year passed, Minerva became more and more infuriatingly hard to resist. He wanted to reach out and drag her back into his arms to show her how much he cared for her. Instead, Anthony crossed his arms over his chest, secured his fingers tightly beneath his triceps, and counted.

One-one thousand.

Two-one thousand.

Three-one thousand.

Four-one thousand.

For as long as he'd known her, five seconds was the longest stretch of silence Minerva would allow. He stared into her pretty hazel eyes. "I should have known better than to involve Kent. I presume it was your brother who has alerted you that I'm about to depart shortly."

Brow creased, Minerva asked, "Why didn't you tell me yourself?"

His hands flew out wide. "How was I supposed to do that when you've been avoiding me!" He glared down at her.

Her cheeks pinkened, but her gaze remained trained on him. He searched her features, features that he could draw blindfolded. Guilt. She was guilty as a fox. The minx was a master chess player and had outmaneuvered him for the past three months. But here she was. In his bedroom questioning him. He should be the one demanding answers for her behavior, not the other way round.

"I've not risked my reputation this eve to enter into an unwanted argument with you," she said.

"Then please share…why are you here?"

Minerva took a half step closer. "Is it your wish to leave your home? Your friends?"

"You know it's not."

"Then why not appease the Head of the Foreign Office and challenge me to a game of chess? After all, it's highly unlikely that you shall win."

Minerva's brazen declaration stabbed him in the chest. It was his own bloody fault for letting her believe a lie. A lie that had been festering under his skin for years. "And what if I did win?"

"You won't." Minerva stepped around him and peered out the window, her breath fogging up the glass.

"Minerva?"

She didn't turn to face him. She was avoiding him, which meant there was a possibility she wasn't as confident at a victory despite her boastful claims.

One-one thousand.

Two-one thousand.

Three-one thousand.

Four-one thousand.

Five-one thousand.

On cue, Minerva said, "I defeated you soundly once before, and I shall easily trounce you again."

The woman was hitting a nerve. He had forfeited the damn game. Not that he'd ever let her know that. But if he were to play her again, wanting her, desiring her, he might not have the willpower to let her win once more. And if he were honest, her winning would be the only satisfactory outcome, for he couldn't marry her.

"You didn't answer my question," he said. "What if I were to win?"

"I would agree to you marry you, of course. After all, that is what I declared, remember?"

Oh, he remembered. In a moment of pure panic and jealousy

during her debut Season, he had subtly goaded her into making the absurd challenge to marry the man who could best her in a game of chess. At the time, he hadn't realized how torturous it would be for him to watch her play gentleman after gentleman, willing her to win every match. Nor had he anticipated the toll it would take on Minerva. If he could travel back in time, he would have ignored Kent's concerns over Minerva's prospects during her debut Season, and for certain would never have shared with Kent the idiotic idea of a challenge.

Minerva turned around but did not meet his gaze and added, "You need not worry. I have no intention of losing. I have my own plans…for my future, and they do not include wedlock."

"I heard you intend to journey to America for a spell."

"My brother really needs to learn to keep family matters a secret, especially since Isadora will be marrying an agent for the Foreign Office."

"Humor me. Suppose I challenge you and, due to a stroke of good luck, I am able to defeat you. Would you marry me of your own free will, and not because you declared you would to all and sundry?"

Minerva's hands fisted at her hips. "I professed I'd willingly marry the man who defeated me. What more do you want from me?"

He swallowed his first response—a declaration of love—and shook his head. "I don't know what I want anymore."

"Do you want to board the *Quarter Moon* in the morn?"

"No."

She finally raised her chin so that their eyes met. "Then why not fight for what you want for once? You've always claimed you never wished to venture abroad. It was why you declined to work for the Foreign Office, time and time again." She stepped up and reached out to take his hand. "If you truly desire to remain on English soil, then I suggest you challenge me to a game of chess. But we must conduct the chess match in private. I don't want anyone, especially my family, to know about our match."

Minerva sighed. "I guess there would have to be one exception…we would have to inform the Head of the Foreign Office, since they instigated this debacle."

"In private? Impossible. There are too many who are already aware of my predicament. If I remain, your brother, Isadora, Avondale, and his sister all will assume I have challenged you to a match."

"Hmm… You would make a terrible spy, with your inability to keep anything a secret."

Ha. Little did she know he did have secrets—like his true feelings for her. "Why are you so certain you shall win?"

Minerva countered, "Why do you believe there's a chance you could win?"

He was running out of patience. Anthony lowered his tone and growled. "Minerva."

In typical Minerva fashion, she pointed her index finger in the air. "First, you haven't played in years." Adding another finger, she continued, "Second, with all the swell you have consumed, I'm certain you've damaged more than a few brain cells, and third, I never lose." It was her turn to search his features. She released his hand. "You're worried I'll not try to defeat you and trap you into marriage?" She placed her hands behind her back and puffed out her chest. "Let me assure you, my lord, I have no interest in marrying you or any other gentleman of my acquaintance. If you don't want my help to ensure you are not shipped off at first light, simply say so and I shall leave."

Damn the woman. She was simultaneously infuriating and desirable. There was no doubt in his mind that he was capable of placing her in check and winning, but she deserved a family of her own. And that was the one thing he could not give her.

For years he had witnessed the glow that would appear around her when she was surrounded by her siblings, and every time he would imagine a gaggle of mini Minervas tugging at her skirts. His heart would fill until hurt. The thought of being thousands of miles away from her was killing him.

He wasn't certain how it all came about, but he had found himself cornered into an impossible situation. But Minerva was right—it was time he pursued what he desired.

"Lady Minerva Malbury, I challenge you to a game of chess—do you accept?"

All the color drained from her cheeks. "I do."

She was scared. He was too.

He traced a finger along her jawline and tipped her chin up. The uncertainty in her eyes crushed his soul. Where was his brave, brazen bluestocking?

He dropped his hand to his side and said, "It is your wish for our game to be conducted in secret."

Minerva nodded.

He loved her—faults and all. To play in secret had a variety of risks and pitfalls for them both. But he could make it possible. He could grant her this one wish.

"Very well. I shall inform the Head of the Foreign Office of our match personally. Then I'll relocate to a dwelling on the east side and let everyone believe I've left Town. Will you be able to sneak out to conduct the game until completion?"

Eyes wide, Minerva stared up at him. "You intend to reside in the shadows for the duration of our match? You would do that for me?" She was fully aware of his preference for company. He hated being alone.

Before he could change his mind, he walked over to the side table next to his bed and retrieved a piece of parchment, quill, and ink. He penned the address of the residence he had let out for years. The location many believed belonged to a mistress that was in fact nonexistent. In order to deflect questions, Anthony had kept up the appearance of maintaining a fake mistress for years, even talked and complained about her as if she were real. It was quite astonishing how simple it was to fool others with very little evidence.

An image of the infamous Madame Rose flashed before him. His brief but intense interlude with the opera singer was the only instance where he had even considered the idea of a mistress. Except when he had closed his eyes with the willing woman in his arms, all he pictured was Minerva. It was as if in his mind, the two women were one.

He shook his head to clear his muddled thoughts and handed Minerva the address. "It shall be a challenge to live in Town in secret—however, if we work together, it shouldn't be too hard a feat, wouldn't you agree?"

Minerva took the note from him and tapped the corner of the parchment against his chest. "A challenge for you, mayhap, but not for I." Her cheeks regained some of their color and the corner of her lips curved into an almost smile. "It takes at least a six months by ship to reach India. Even if we limited ourselves to one move per player, per night, it would take at most three weeks to complete. How will you explain your early reappearance?"

Her keen intelligence had his heart aflutter. He loved how their thoughts mirrored each other the majority of the time. Having considered the scenario mere moments ago, he answered, "Rough seas, boat repair—there are a number of reasons for the voyage to be canceled. Or we could extend the game so only one player may move each night…" If the intel that Minerva intended to leave for America in three weeks was correct, she would balk at his proposal.

"I see no need to prolong your suffering. If you are not worried about wagging tongues on your sudden return, then I suggest we complete the game as quickly as possible. Then we each can move on."

She'd thrown down the gauntlet. His pride bucked at the idea of his forfeiting their match, but he wouldn't deny her a life with children. He might not be able to seize victory, but he could play a game that would challenge her…a game she wouldn't forget.

"It will take me a day to disappear. We can begin our game two nights hence?" he asked.

Her eyes narrowed as she read the address on the parchment. "Will we be alone when playing?"

Out of habit, he continued with his lie about his fake mistress. "The residence is currently vacant and has been for a few months."

"Very well. I shall see you there." Minerva crumpled the parchment and threw it into the fire.

He wasn't ready for her to leave. When she turned back to face him, he caved in to his desires, pulled her close, and crushed his lips to hers to seal their deal.

With her arms linked around his neck, her fingertips brushed the sensitive skin just above the material of his cravat. Minerva returned his kisses.

She was kissing him back.

This wasn't her first kiss.

A ball of rage and jealousy rolled through him. Who in the devil's name had dared to touch her so intimately?

He pulled back as his mind raced. "I'll escort you home."

Confusion and then anger flared in her eyes. "There's no need. I don't need your help."

"Ah, but I need yours." He presented his arm for her, but the minx ignored him and marched out of his chambers without a backward glance.

Rooted to the spot, he let her go.

There was something oddly familiar about the way her tongue had caressed his. Oh, he had fantasized and dreamt about kissing Minerva numerous times, but he'd never dared to kiss his best friend's sister…until tonight. His mind was playing tricks on him.

He flopped on the bed and closed his eyes. He needed a respite before having to deal with the Head of the Foreign Office.

CHAPTER FOUR

T RAPPED IN HER private study for two full days and two extremely long evenings with her sister Isadora and Charlotte nattering on and on was all Minerva could tolerate. She was close to losing her composure and behaving in a manner that would prove to one and all that she was not in fact an Ice Queen. Except she couldn't bear the thought of causing her sister and her soon-to-be sister-in-law's smiles to disappear. A few more days and the plans for her sister's engagement party would be well in hand.

Minerva pressed her fingers to her temples and tuned out the voices about her. It had taken her twice as long as she expected to organize what should have been a simple dinner party. However, when your sister was to marry a duke, who was acquainted with more than half the *ton*, compiling the guestlist was a feat in itself. Normally such tasks would not have proven a challenge, but with Charlotte and Isadora insisting on conducting a discussion and evaluation of each gentleman's character and qualities before adding them to the list, the process was long and arduous. It didn't help that Minerva mentally compared each one of the men to Anthony.

Minerva dropped her hands to her lap and stared at the large pile of invitations that needed to be stuffed into envelopes. Two weeks until her sister married a duke, an agent for the Foreign

Office. Two weeks until she would be free of her immediate family obligations. With Gregory busy at university and Paul completing his senior year at Eton, there was nothing stopping her from pursuing her dreams. Yes, in two weeks she could finally embark upon an adventure of her own.

In better spirits, she began to hum as she picked up an envelope and mindlessly jammed an invitation inside.

She was on her third invite when Anthony's image appeared as she blinked. Blast the man. Her plans would have to wait. Wait until…until she defeated the man who had destroyed her self-preserving promises of never loving him again with the brush of his lips.

Gah! She had best formulate a sound plan for sneaking out then journeying across Town in quick succession. She needed to complete their chess game in no more than fourteen days or she would jeopardize her plans for the Season.

A knot formed in her stomach. The idea of venturing across Town to a residence that no doubt had previously housed Anthony's mistress had her heart breaking. She didn't want to see, let alone occupy, a room where Anthony had made love to another.

Her hand shook as she reached for another invitation. She released a sigh. *Get a hold of yourself.*

She glanced over at Isadora, who was thankfully preoccupied, listening intently to yet another one of Charlotte's childhood stories. Minerva supposed it was only natural Charlotte adored her much older brother, since they were parentless. The way the girl went on about her older brother, Isadora's husband-to-be, you would think the Duke of Aces was a saint and not the devilish soul who took risks for the sake of king and country.

Risks.

She too was guilty of taking risks that most would claim were too great. After all, there was no greater risk than the one she was taking by playing Anthony. After mulling over the chess match she had played with him years ago, she had a sinking feeling that the man might have tricked her. Tricked her into believing she had won fair and square, when, in fact, Anthony had forfeited the game on purpose. What was riskier—being all alone with Drake and wanting his lips on her again, or the growing self-doubt that she might not be able to defeat the man as easily as she had claimed?

The edge of an invitation sliced the tip of her finger, and she reached for another. "Ouch." Before blood could ruin the parchment, Minerva stuck her finger in her mouth.

"Whose invitation dared to injure you, sister?" Isadora's grin was hard to ignore. Avondale, of all the gentlemen in the world, made her sister annoyingly happy.

Minerva peered at Avondale's bold script. Her future brother-in-law, Tom—the poor man would have to learn not to wager with Isadora, or he'd find himself in charge of the dinner menu and any other task Isadora deplored.

Minerva smiled as she read the invitee's name and replied, "It was the honorable Viscount Northwell." Northwell? The man was notorious for his candid remarks and held the record for being tossed from various assemblies and balls. Isadora must have added him to list without discussion.

Charlotte coughed and failed to cover her laughter. "Would you consider Northwell a worthy opponent if he were to challenge you to a chess match?"

"That is the fourth gentleman you have inquired about to-day." Minerva held out her hand and said, "Hand me that invitation list."

Isadora handed over the list. Minerva scanned the names, many she was certain hadn't been discussed or agreed upon. She mentally counted. Three-quarters of the list were gentlemen, and of those, half were part of Avondale's set that had devoutly declared bachelorhood. "Sister, etiquette would state you invite an equal ratio of ladies to gentleman. What are you scheming?"

"I'm merely attempting to become better acquainted with my fiancé's friends," Isadora replied.

It would take too long to extract the truth from her sister, so Minerva shifted her attention directly upon Charlotte. "Pray, explain why there is a distinct lack of eligible ladies from the Wicked Ladies Salon."

Charlotte gave her a sweet smile and replied, "We can't afford to lose more members this early in the Season—terrible for morale. As you know, part of the allure of being a member of the salon is to mingle with ladies of similar determination to remain unwed."

Minerva had no counterargument. A first for her. She glanced down at the list and read off the first name that caught her attention. "The Earl of Camdon? I've read about the man, but he's been a ghost about Town."

Charlotte's nose crinkled. "He's recently returned from the Continent."

"The Continent? Was he enlisted?"

"No."

Charlotte and Isadora shared a look, and it was Isadora who said, "He's an agent for the Crown, specifically with the Foreign Office."

"Do you know him well, Charlotte?"

"Well enough." The girl was never short on words. Her curt responses indicated she knew far more about the man than she was willing to admit.

A housemaid rolled in a tea cart and positioned it in the center of the room. Charlotte hopped up and grabbed a lemon tart and popped it in her mouth.

Minerva stacked the sealed invitations into a pile and whispered, "You won't succeed."

"Succeed?" Isadora asked.

"Aye, your scheme to marry me off to one of Avondale's friends will fail for multiple reasons, but primarily because I wish to have no affiliations with the Crown and the bloody Foreign Office."

"Why?"

Minerva couldn't admit it was for purely selfish reasons. She didn't want the responsibility of others, and she'd spent most of her years taking care of or prioritizing others before herself. Free from those responsibilities, she wanted to live a different life. One that didn't bind her by social rules. One that allowed her to express herself...

She wanted to live as her alter ego, Madame Rose. The mysterious opera singer that was highly sought after on both sides of the channel.

Minerva squared her shoulders, feigning disinterest at the topic at hand, and prepared to answer. "Having you and Avondale involved is more than enough for one family."

"But you have skills and abilities that they obviously seek." It was clear Isadora was not done discussing the issue.

Minerva calmly replied, "You possess many of those same skills. I have other pursuits I wish to fulfill."

"Mayhap if you shared those with me, I could assist and persuade the decision makers in the Foreign Office to leave you alone."

Isadora's words hit a nerve. Minerva didn't need help. She managed an entire household, kept the family together as one, and...and now she was ready to be alone.

Forcing her lips to form a smile, Minerva said, "Sister mine, focus on your upcoming nuptials and stop trying to play matchmaker."

Charlotte returned, tea in hand. "There must be at least one if not two gentlemen upon the list that you find interesting."

Minerva glanced at the list of names once more. If she didn't play along, then the pair would only devise another scheme. At least this one she could manipulate to her advantage—draw attention away from her real plans and provide her with alibis for evenings when she needed to venture out to play Drake. It would be far easier to disappear for an hour or two during an event than to have to sneak out of the Malbury townhouse night after night.

She spotted a name that brought a frown. "Why does Mr.

Scott's name not resonate?"

"He is the brother of the Marquess of Dunbury, who is also on the guestlist," Isadora replied.

"Dunbury…Dunbury… Ah, I recall the gentleman now." Did her sister not know of his advanced age? Dunbury was at least twice Minerva's age.

As if her sister had read her mind, Isadora said, "We were considering mayhap a man of his years and experience might actually be—"

Charlotte intervened. "Dunbury might prove to be a worthy opponent. He's known to be well versed at the game of chess. Mr. Scott is easy on the eyes and is purported to be a fair player himself."

"Hmmm…perhaps it will prove to be an interesting evening, full of possibilities." Minerva gathered the stack and walked over to Jack, her most trusted footman, who had assisted her and her sisters on a number of occasions over the summer. The footman was dependable, loyal, and, best of all, remained silent on all of their escapades. Minerva handed the invitations to him and said, "Please see that these are delivered." She glanced about to make sure Isadora and Charlotte were preoccupied before continuing, "Can you also arrange to have a hack at the ready for later this eve? I shall need the conveyance to and from…from a friend's residence."

"I shall see to it, my lady. I'm assuming I'll be accompanying you on your visit."

Minerva nodded, and Jack left.

Isadora was studying Minerva very closely. Minerva knew it would be best not to rush to execute her plans and attempt to live a double life…so for now she would join her sister and future sister-in-law for tea and act as if she was seriously contemplating adhering to the social norm for a daughter of the peerage, who were all doomed to marry and produce an heir and a spare.

Bah. Life as Madame Rose was what she desired—except the image of Drake and a miniature version of Drake flashed before her, and her heart fluttered. She shook her head—marrying Drake had been a childhood fantasy. She was no longer young and naïve. The man had made it clear it wasn't marriage he was opposed to…it was marriage to her that he wouldn't consider, and she wasn't about to place her heart in danger of being hurt again by him.

CHAPTER FIVE

ORTY-EIGHT HOURS SHOULD have been more than enough time for the sweet taste of Minerva's lips to have dissipated, yet Anthony found himself licking his bottom lip and reliving the kiss that he had intended to leave her longing for more—but it was he who was left wanting. Damn the woman. When it came to Minerva, his ability to predict a person's next move vanished, became nonexistent…and it was damn annoying. The woman's actions were as unpredictable as her chess play.

He pulled out his pocket watch and rubbed his thumb over the slightly marred glass face—ten past one in the morning. Argh. Minerva was late.

The dusty, outdated drapes covering the windows of his normally vacant townhouse, which was rumored to house his nonexistent mistress, were sheer enough to view the road outside. Hands clenched tightly behind his back, he scanned the main thoroughfare. No sign of Minerva. Eyes closed, he listened for the sound of horse hooves, but instead his ears were subjected to the bawdy shouts of young chaps making their way to the hell house that was a few doors down.

Five more minutes.

If Minerva failed to appear in four minutes and forty-five seconds, he swore he would go in search of her and then wring her neck for making him worry.

A barely detectable draft of cold air fueled the fire, sending the flames in the sparsely decorated receiving room higher for a moment. He carefully scanned the room. No one, not even a creature, was in sight. The exposed skin at the back of his neck continued to tingle. He turned his attention back to the window. Damnation, where was Minerva?

Three minutes.

Eyed closed once more, he inhaled deeply and forced himself not to fidget. The scent of flowers gave away Minerva's presence, yet he still flinched at the light tap on his shoulder.

He stiffened as he turned to face Minerva. His body prepared for an attack, but it wasn't a physical altercation that he protected himself from—it was the onslaught of emotions that Minerva caused within him. Even in the dark, he was able to admire her beautiful features.

He cleared his throat and said, "That is twice now that you have managed to sneak up on me. Pray tell, how do you do it?"

Minerva pushed back the hood of her cloak. "I haven't come to share my secrets, I'm here to play a game and save you from an extended trip abroad." She stripped out of her gloves and cloak and shoved them at his chest.

So much for formalities or greetings or the hope of another kiss. Minerva was obviously in a rush to be done and return to whatever *ton* event she had snuck away from.

He placed her discarded items on the arm of the settee. Of course, it was unreasonable of him to expect she would want to spend the rest of the evening with him. She was not here to be ravished. She was here to save him from being banished to reside on the other side of the planet.

He followed her as she strode over to the chessboard he had set up in front of the fireplace. Without hesitation she picked up one light-colored and one-dark colored pawn, placed one in each hand, turned to face him, and wound her arms behind her. "Choose."

If he picked the lighter-colored pawn, he would go first, giving him a miniscule mathematical advantage over Minerva. Had she switched the pawns behind her back, or had she simply kept the white in her right hand? It wasn't a difficult decision; he simply needed to pick. But he desperately wanted the advantage. He nodded and said, "Right."

She brought an arm around and unfurled the fingers of her right hand, palm face up. She rolled the dark-colored pawn back and forth, taunting him. Damn.

Minerva wouldn't let the advantage go to waste. Her first move would set the tone for their game, but if her trickery, switching pawns behind her back, was any indication, Anthony was in for a devilishly hard match.

She returned the pieces to the board, and Anthony pulled out her chair for her. Minerva slipped gracefully into her seat. "I've never seen a set quite like this one." She picked up the king and slowly twirled it between her fingers to study the piece closely.

"I believe it originates from Germany." He took his own seat and repositioned the pieces out of habit rather than necessity.

Minerva picked up the knight topped with a horse's head rather than the traditional notched collar. "How lovely. When and how did you come by such a lovely set?"

"I won it at the tables." Anthony waited for Minerva to begin.

She replaced the knight on the board and peered at him. "Why would you wager for such an exquisite chess set when you don't play?"

He wasn't ready to admit how often he played while alone with this very set, when others believed him to be preoccupied with an imaginary mistress. Instead, he replied, "I like to win no matter what the prize is." His reply garnered a smile from Minerva.

He needed to be closer to her. He slid his chair in and leaned forward, resting his hands on his knees, and waited. Waited for her to begin their game.

"Whom did you win it from?"

Apparently, she wasn't in as much of a hurry to leave as he

first thought. "A fellow peer."

"Ah, I see you are set on keeping your secrets." Minerva picked up a pawn and studied it for a moment. "Shall we make the game a tad more interesting?"

"You want to wager more than your word to marry?"

She continued to study the chess piece, which was worrisome.

Wary of raising the stakes, yet curious, Anthony asked, "What do you propose?"

Lips curved into a smile, Minerva answered, "Every time I place you in check, you shall share one of your secrets, and vice versa."

The odds were not in his favor. But if his calculations were correct, there was only a slim chance Minerva would place him in check more than once. He could afford to give up one secret.

The glint in her eyes gave him pause. Maybe one secret was too much. He had watched every game she'd played over the past three Seasons, and many more before that. First to act, she would adopt a very aggressive attack strategy. Would he be able to mount a counter-defense?

Betting on his skill, Anthony replied, "Rather than the person in check deciding what secret to divulge, may I suggest they must answer a specific query instead." He wanted to confirm if Minerva's plans included traveling abroad or if it was all a ruse.

With a decisive nod, Minerva placed her pawn two spaces forward.

If they were only to play one move each time they met, the evening would be over as soon as he made his move. Not ready for Minerva to leave, he stared at the board and weighed his options. Go aggressive or make a defensive first move?

The susurrus of Minerva's skirts interrupted his thoughts, which were quickly replaced by vivid images of her bare thigh. Not that he'd ever seen her bare thigh, but he had frequently fantasized about her naked. If he didn't rein in his imagination, he'd find himself reaching over the board and toppling its pieces to kiss her.

Damn. Double damn.

He should be guarding his best friend's sister's reputation, not placing it in jeopardy. It was imperative she not be seen by one of their peers in this part of Town. If he cared about her as he claimed, then he needed to act. Make his move.

His hand hovered over the row of pawns, moving left to right and back to the left again. He could mirror her move, which was most likely what she expected him to do, or he could move his rook's pawn a single space, which she would consider a mistake on his part and a huge boon for her. Anthony opted for the latter.

Minerva stood with her hands on her hips, her gaze focused on the board separating them. "What a surprising move on your part. If this is the level of play I should expect from you, my dear friend, the game shall be over in…"

She tapped her chin with her forefinger, a habit that drove Anthony to distraction. However, her emphasis on the word *friend* clearly reminded him that that was all he was to her…a friend, a friend she was helping out.

Minerva made her way across the room to the settee where he'd placed outer garments. "…a fortnight." She slid her hand into a glove and wiggled her fingers, and Anthony had to swallow the lump that had formed in his throat. Who knew donning gloves could be so evocative?

Minerva slipped on the other glove and added, "Yes. It shall take me no more than a fortnight to claim victory. Then you shall be able to emerge from the shadows."

Victory? Shadows? He blinked to refocus his wayward mind. "Will you be able to return tomorrow?" Anthony held his breath as he shook out her cloak for her.

Minerva stepped closer, and he wrapped the thick material about her shoulders. Face to face he wanted to experience her lips upon his once more, but he stepped back, placing a good foot between them. She was his best friend's sister, not a paramour to dally with. No matter how strong her pull was, he had to refrain from kissing her again. Having been taunted by the taste of her for two days, he might not succeed at stopping or being satisfied with only a kiss.

She looped the ribbons of her cloak and tied a knot. "Not tomorrow. I'm to attend a private dinner party with Isadora, Charlotte, and Avondale at Lord Camdon's residence."

"Camdon?" When in the blazes had the man returned to England?

"That is what I said—Lord Camdon. What do you know of him?" Minerva peered up at him with a twinkle of interest in her eyes. "Isadora believes he might be a worthy challenger, but Charlotte's information on the man was unusually sparse, which I surmise means the man is not that worthy."

Camdon had been one of Anthony's closer friends at university—that was, until he was recruited by the Foreign Office and shipped off to the Continent. Anthony had corresponded with Camdon on a number of occasions over the years. He had lived vicariously through his friend's missions from the safety of his home. It would be grand to be able to visit with his old friend.

Why had he agreed to play the match in secret?

Ah, yes, for the simple fact that Minera had wished it so. Living in the shadows was not his cup of tea. Living in solitary for two days had already proven to be rather tiresome and extremely lonely. The two things he constantly worked hard to avoid.

The tap of Minerva's toe brought his attention back to her. He smiled and said, "I would agree with Isadora that he could be a worthy opponent, but I also agree with Charlotte: the man is a chameleon. Hard to know who he really is."

"Hmm…then tomorrow shall prove to be a rather interesting eve. I plan to escape from the Harmon Ball the following eve, and if our game moves as swiftly as tonight, I should be able to return without issue." Minerva walked to the door.

He followed and held the door open for her. "Who's to attend the Harmon event?"

As she passed over the threshold, she said, "Everyone."

Everyone? The vague response raised the hairs on the back of his neck.

He peered out into the hall. Minerva was gone. He raced back to look out the front window. There were no vehicles in the street. How in the devil did the minx appear and disappear like magic?

CHAPTER SIX

S KIRTS GRIPPED TIGHTLY in her hands and hiked above her ankles, Minerva raced out the back door. She nearly ran over Jack, who was sitting on the bottom stoop waiting for her. Thankfully, the footman popped up and stood to attention.

"Let's be off." Minerva slowed her pace once she entered the back alley. What a fool she had been to attempt to goad Anthony into action with jealousy. The tactic had already proven ineffective once before. And yet his calm response to her dining with Lord Camdon, who was reportedly both dashing and extremely blessed with a sharp mind, set her blood on fire. Embarrassment roared through her veins. Anthony hadn't issued the challenge because he wanted to marry her; it was simply to avoid banishment. What a ninny she was to believe the kiss, the kiss that had her lying awake all night, meant something to him.

Argh. The man was insufferable.

Jack lengthened his stride and stepped up to walk alongside her. "My lady…is everythin' all right? Should we alter our plans for the rest of the evening?" He glanced over his shoulder and then back to her. "Perhaps it's best if we return…"

"No. The plan remains the same." Minerva tugged her cloak tighter about her shoulders, warding off the nonexistent chill in the air. She hastened her steps, ready to complete the next task on her list for the evening—secure her own private lodgings for the

Season.

While her feet were moving forward, her mind remained focused on Anthony. She shouldn't have given in to temptation the other night. He regretted their kiss. He must, or he would have kissed her again when he had helped her with her cloak.

Her heels struck the pavement as the bitter taste of rejection settled in. "Let's locate a hack and proceed to our meeting." She squeezed the material clutched at her chest. Sneaking about Town wasn't what had her worried; it was the man whom she intended to meet. A man who had the ability to threaten the success of her plans—Mr. Wembley. The shrewd man managed a great number of properties around Town, including the quarters above the playhouse Minerva wished to let for a year.

"Are you certain Mr. Wembley can be trusted?"

Her footman's concern mirrored her own. Isadora's dealings with Mr. Wembley in the past proved he wasn't the most trustworthy man. She shook her head. "I have no choice but to trust the man. I'll admit that Mr. Wembley does pose the greatest threat to my plans for the Season. I can only hope that the man continues to be driven by greed and not sense." She had agreed to pay the man double the letting fee in order to buy his silence.

No one could find out she intended to spend an entire Season as her alter ego Madame Rose. The only person privy to her true plans was Jack, and she trusted him with her life daily. Her family believed she was to act as companion to dear old Aunt Adelaide, who was journeying across the pond. Minerva didn't in fact wish to leave England and venture so far away, and since Aunt Adelaide already secretly had a companion, her aunt had been more than happy to go along with the ruse.

They exited the alley, and Jack put his fingers to his mouth. The loud whistle caught the attention of a hansom driver down the street. As the vehicle rolled to a stop in front of them, Jack said, "Lady Minerva, it's not too late to change your mind."

It had taken years to train Jack to speak his mind, and he'd proven to be an excellent judge of character, possessing knowledge beyond her gilded cage that had proven invaluable many times. "My mind is set. Let's be off."

Jack shook his head as he assisted her up into the hack. Alone, Minerva closed her eyes and inhaled deeply as she rested her forehead against the cool glass of the window.

The image of Anthony appeared like always when she closed her eyes. Why could she not simply stop caring for the blasted man? Her dreams of his returning her regard after all these years should well and truly be dead. Yet they unrelentingly lingered.

The man who had captured her heart as a young teen was a rogue. According to Benedict, Anthony was no stranger to kissing women. Yet he hadn't attempted to kiss her again. Which told her their kiss the other night meant nothing to him, while it had certainly meant something to her. She wanted to forget the soul-awakening kiss after having lost far too many hours of sleep reimagining the man's lips upon hers. Why was her heart so stubborn?

She released the captured breath and sat back to peer out the foggy window. Finishing their chess match post haste was the best plan moving forward. It was time for her to focus on her own future. She would assume her alter ego's identity.

Minerva's lips curved into a smile. Becoming Madame Rose would allow her to shed all societal restriction of being a lady for an entire Season. One Season of adventure. One Season as someone the complete opposite of the Ice Queen. Yes, one Season, and then she'd return to her staid life as a spinster and hopefully become the favored aunt to her siblings' children, much like Aunt Adelaide had been to her.

Anthony's image appeared in the glass, haunting her. He was the only man she wanted to marry. For three Seasons she had tried to entertain the idea of marrying another. But with her mind bored with trivial conversations and the lack of fluttering in her chest, Minerva had given up hope. She resolved to never marry, but she wanted one extravagant adventure for herself. Planning such an elaborate charade had been her only salvation the past few years.

She should be both excited and pleased with her progress, yet her chess match with Anthony was a distraction. All the years of gathering the right contacts and planning were all coming together. She was going to live a life she had longed for. Not bound by societal rules of the *ton*. Free to explore.

No more pining. It was time for action.

Refocused on her mission, she peered out the window again. They were no longer on the outskirts of Mayfair. Her breath caught in her chest and her palms began to sweat. Would she be able to manage on her own? Having lived under her father's roof, protected by Benedict and surrounded by staff and family, Minerva found the idea of living alone had a certain appeal.

Alone. Anthony's two days of isolation had resulted in the man peering out the window like a hound waiting for its master to return. Only Anthony hadn't greeted her with as much enthusiasm as what her dogs did.

Bah. To hell with the man.

They weren't far from the playhouse. Hurriedly, she pushed back her hood and reached into her cloak pocket for the small compact case of powder. With swift, practiced movements, she patted a sponge with the white cake along the bridge of her nose, over her cheeks, along her forehead, and finished with swipes over her jawline. She flipped over the case and extracted the black dot that she placed on her upper left cheek. She didn't have time to kohl her eyes, but if she kept her hood low over her eyes, Mr. Wembley should be none the wiser.

The doors to the playhouse came into view, and her pulse quickened. She pressed her lips tightly together and grazed her teeth over her bottom lip to bring color to it. A jolt of energy and excitement replaced her worries, and she shifted to the edge of her seat. When Jack opened the door for her, she was ready. Ready to embark on the next phase of her plan.

Minerva hopped down with the assistance of Jack's hand. "Isn't it grand!"

"It's definitely something, my lady." Jack's dark frown returned. "Allow me to accompany you inside."

"If I'm to live as I plan, I must become accustomed to doing things on my own." She patted his arm and reassured him, "All will be well."

Her gaze landed on the rickety stairwell that led to the lodgings up above, up to the room she would call home for several months. She ventured along the hard-packed dirt path that led to the back door of the playhouse, making sure she didn't come too close to the drab brown boards that were a stark contrast to the whitewashed brick of the Malbury townhouse. Minerva clasped her gloved hand over her nose and mouth as the stench of ale and vomit assaulted her. She shuffled the remaining few feet and reached the foot of the stairs.

What was she waiting for?

She glanced over her shoulder to find Jack loitering close by. Every ounce of courage she thought she'd possessed mysteriously vanished. The urge to abandon her plans and forfeit her match to Anthony nearly had her turning and running back toward her footman.

No.

Three years of planning.

Three years of dreaming of a different life.

Three years of negotiations were not going to go to waste.

She planted her foot on the first step and then climbed the rest in quick succession before she changed her mind. Knuckles poised inches from the door, Minerva mumbled, "If Mr. Wembley is inside…then Madam Rose I shall become." She puffed out her chest and rapped on the door three times in quick succession, followed by a pause, and then three more knocks against the thin wooden door. The hollow knocks reverberated through the tight alley and her. "If he's already left…then I shall—"

Her negative thoughts flew from her mind as the door whooshed open.

Mr. Wembley appeared with a dark scowl upon his dour

features. "Madame. You. Are. Late."

Lips curled into a lopsided smile, Minerva replied, "Ahh... Mr. Wembley, the night is still young." She added a singsong lilt to her voice that sounded rusty to her own ears.

Minerva strode into the room, her heart bursting with joy. The room was large, unusually large, and it had windows on two of the walls. Two, which was one more than her current bedroom had. Sunshine during the day. Privacy at night. It was perfect. A space all of her own.

She scanned the space, which was bare of furnishings. Where did one purchase a bed and linens and such?

"The letting fee is two shillings a week, eight for the month, in advance first of the month." Mr. Wembley held out his hand.

She reached into her cloak, extracted a half-sovereign, and handed it over. "I'd like to take possession tonight. The extra should cover any inconvenience to you."

Palm up, Mr. Wembley bobbed his hand up and down, assessing the coin's weight. Then he popped his hand into his waistcoat and extracted a key. "I'll be back next month for the rent."

Without a farewell, the grumpy old man walked out of the room, leaving her alone.

She meandered over to the window and peered down at the alley. Jack was pacing back and forth, still shaking his head. Her footman would know where and how to obtain the items she needed. She hoped she'd extorted enough of her sisters' pin money to afford at least a bed and clean linens. They were additional costs not factored into her original plan.

What other obstacles would she face?

She twirled in a circle. Privacy.

Eyes closed, she imagined decorating the room to her own tastes. Yes. This would become her space, and it would all be worth it. If she wasn't able to obtain her dream of a love match and children, then her childhood fantasy of being an actress upon the stage was the next best thing.

CHAPTER SEVEN

Anthony tugged his gloves off and sank down on Minerva's empty bed.

Where the bloody hell was she? The slap of leather against his thighs punctuated his disbelief. Having regretted letting her leave so soon, he had hailed a hack and followed her home. He was no stranger to the Malbury townhouse, but creeping through the halls in the middle of the night and entering Minerva's chambers was new. Not too long ago, he and Kent would return to the Malbury townhouse half foxed after a long night of revelry. Now that Kent was a happily married man, those days were over.

Back on his feet, Anthony went to the window. With no trellis and no tree close by, the only way Minerva could reenter was through the door. At least she wouldn't be able to sneak up on him this time.

He paced the width of her room.

Why had he chased after her?

To confess his feelings for her. No, he couldn't do that.

To kiss her senseless. No, he most certainly could not do that either.

Damnation. Mid-stride, he stopped. What if Minerva had been kidnapped?

He swiveled and headed for the door. How careless of him not to have seen her home safely. He didn't deserve her regard the way he had mistreated her.

His heart raced. If she was lost to him, she'd never know how he really felt. How he'd been madly in love with her since their very first chess match. Damn, he was a dunderhead. What he needed to do was go find her and never let her out of his sight again.

He took two paces toward the door and froze. The soft patter of footsteps in the hall was barely detectable. Minerva had returned.

Anthony shifted to wait against the wall. His heart clamored in his chest. He needed to make certain she was unharmed, but he also did not wish to startle her. After slow, deep breaths, his pulse resumed its normal steady pace. In the dark he tapped his fingers against his thigh, counting out the seconds before the door latch rattled.

Remain calm. Don't rush.

He pressed his back against the wall, and the door slowly opened. Instead of rushing in, Minerva peered into the room. Thankfully, the door partially hid him from her. Had she sensed his presence? If she had, she gave him no indication she knew he was waiting for her.

Minerva slipped in and leaned up against the door. Eyes closed, she rested her head back and sighed. It was a sigh of exhaustion. What the devil had she been up to?

He wouldn't find out by remaining hidden in the shadows. A long stride, and a quick turn, and he stepped in front of her and covered her mouth with his hand.

Her eyes popped open wide and then narrowed.

He quickly whispered, "Shh. You wouldn't want to wake up Gregory or Isadora, now, would you?"

She hadn't bitten him or tried to shove him off; she simply stared back at him. Concerned at her passive behavior, he removed his hand from her mouth and flipped it over to press it against her forehead. Warm but not fevered.

Satisfied, he took a step back and noticed a whitish mark on the back of his hand. Face paint? Earlier, at his lodgings, Minerva's beautiful face had been devoid of the pasty powder. His mind whirled with more who, what, and why questions.

Minerva walked around him and began to shed her cloak and gloves. A silent Minerva was an angry—a *very* angry Minerva. He knew better than to approach.

She threw her outer garments on her bed and rounded again to face him with her hands on her hips. "What are you doing in my chambers?"

She was clearly unharmed and ready to do battle with him. Before her debut, they'd rarely argued. He missed those days. The days where they talked about everything and anything. The days when he wasn't subjected, on a daily basis, to gentlemen gazing upon her with interest and his having to hide his own feelings for her.

He was done hiding in the shadows. He stepped to get closer and circled her. Answers. That was what he needed. His gaze narrowed on an unusually pale spot at her temple along her hairline. Her cheeks were a shade of pink, as far as he could tell in the dim moonlight. He leaned in closer to peer into her eyes, to make sure she was well, but really the movement was a ploy to get closer. Closer to her lips.

He wished he'd kissed her earlier.

He straightened and clasped his hands behind him, a precaution to prevent his reaching for her and acting upon his desires before he received the answers he came for. "Where in the hell did you venture to after you left my temporary lodgings?"

Chin in the air, she replied, "I shan't be answering any of your questions until you answer mine."

"Very well. I wished to ensure you returned home safely." He averted his gaze from her generous bosom, which was front and center now that her arms were firmly crossed beneath her bustline.

"Since you have verified my return, you may leave."

She tried to sidestep around him again, but he blocked her

path to the door. "First, tell me where you went." He left out the expletive he was sure Minerva had taken exception to earlier.

"I had an errand to see to."

"An errand? In the middle of the night?" He didn't believe her, but he also didn't know what to think. "Did this errand involve visiting another gentleman?" For once, he hoped his intuition was wrong and Minerva's detour before arriving home did not involve another man.

"Not a gentle…man." She was being evasive and would not look him in the eye.

He countered, "A man of any sort?"

"What does it matter to you?" She inched closer, and he took a step back. Moisture gathered in her eyes, but she blinked it away.

Blast, she was upset. He hated that she was unhappy, for he knew her sadness was all his doing.

Minerva spun away from him and faced the window. "The sun shall rise soon. I suggest you leave now, before you lose the advantage of the dark. You wouldn't want to be discovered traipsing through the streets after all the efforts you have taken to hide away for the duration of our chess match, now would you?"

"Actually, I've been debating the advantages and disadvantages of conducting our game in secret, and…"

She turned back around with tears threatening to spill. "And?"

Why was she about to cry?

Women were a complete conundrum, but especially Minerva. He didn't know what he should say next—he merely knew he needed to attempt to explain why he couldn't marry her. "I should have left. Allowed the Head of the Foreign Office to banish me. I shouldn't have issued the challenge to play for your hand. Nothing good can—"

Minerva let out a muffled sob, halting his speech.

He reached out for her, but she whirled out of his reach. "If you regret your decision, then leave!"

If he could leave her, he would, but his heart wouldn't let

him. He moved to stand behind her until he could feel the heat radiating off her back. "Minerva. Hear me out." When she didn't answer, he placed his hands on the tops of her shoulders, needing to be connected to her. He sent up a quick prayer he wouldn't muck up the words he knew that needed to be said. "If you win, I shall be able to feign my return and reenter society, but I'll have to endure a Season of standing in the wings as Isadora and Diana throw gentlemen in your path, and it will only be a matter of time before you deign to grant one of them the privilege of your hand."

She turned, dislodging his hands from her. "I've endured three Seasons, and not once did you express any concern over whether or not I'd marry another. What has changed?"

Everything for him. An ultimatum by the Head of the Foreign Office and the risk of never seeing Minerva again had triggered a need for him to act. He was fully aware that, as he'd summoned her brother to his townhouse three nights ago, Kent would not be able to keep his departure a secret. He knew Minerva would come to his aid. But he still hadn't resolved the issue of the threat to her life if they were to marry.

Hurt-filled eyes stared up at him. She was patiently waiting for an answer. His thoughts scattered into a thousand pieces at the sight of her pain. Pain he had caused. He should stay away from her, but he couldn't do that. He wouldn't do that. For a man who was supposed to be a brilliant strategist, he had certainly made a muck of things with the woman he loved.

"What has changed, you ask…" He employed the same tactic Minerva would use when she needed an extra moment to think.

"Anthony. Simply tell me the truth. Now, out with it."

Ah, at least she wasn't crying, and for the moment she was back to being her bossy, know-it-all self, even if there still remained a tear or two threatening to spill over at the far corners of her eyes.

Best not to delay. "My perspective on our relationship has changed over the course of the last two days. Two days of nothing and no one to distract me led to many, many hours of soul searching."

He sighed and stared down at Minera. It was the truth. Bored to death with his own company, he'd had to face the truth: he wanted to marry Minerva. He simply didn't wish to be the cause of her death.

She raised the back of her hand to her eyes and wiped away the unfallen tears. What was he waiting for? It was time he confessed his true feelings for her.

"Minerva, I…" The words stuck in his throat.

"You what? Regret kissing me? Wished you never issued the challenge? Can't stand the sight of me? What?" She threw her hands in the air and twirled away from him, and then twirled back to confront him.

She was beautiful when she became this passionate.

Minerva jabbed a finger at his shoulder. "If you are so miserable in my company, then leave. Leave this instant." She turned and marched to the door. "And if you are worried that the Head of the Foreign Office shall banish you if we do not finish our chess match, I shall happily agree to completing our game via correspondence. Then you won't have to endure seeing me ever again." She swung the door open and waved a hand, motioning for him to leave.

She believed he didn't want to be in her company when that was *all* he wanted. How could she have misconstrued his intentions? How had he mucked everything up so superbly? Each biting word was like a stab to the chest. She really did not understand how much she meant to him.

Anthony marched to up to stand behind her. He bent to whisper in her ear, "Close the door, Minerva. I wasn't finished explaining."

To his utter surprise, she didn't balk at the order. She didn't turn to glare at him. Minerva quietly did as he asked and pressed her forehead against the wood as the latch fell back into place.

Without her mesmerizing hazel eyes to distract him, he

stepped closer. "You've got it all wrong, my love." Her shoulders stiffened, but he persisted. "I can't stop thinking about our kiss the other night. I no longer care if Kent will hate me for the rest of my days for betraying his trust. I. Love. You. And have done so for many years. Please believe me. I want to win our match, desperately—but I can't marry you."

"I don't understand," Minerva mumbled to the door.

He turned her by the shoulders to face him. "You deserve a loving and devoted husband. A man who won't send you to your grave."

"You think I'll drive you mad and you shall be tempted to commit murder?"

The absurdity of her response made him want to chuckle. But her reply was sincere, stemming from her miserable parents' union, and he didn't want to undermine her fears of enduring such a marriage herself.

He let his hands graze down her arms until he captured her hands in his. "No, this is not about you, Minerva. This about me. About the men in my family."

She blinked up at him. "I'm clearly lacking sleep, for I'm not at all following your logic."

Of course she wasn't—Minerva was an innocent. How was he to explain matters in a gentlemanly manner? He couldn't.

He blurted, "MacMillian men lack strong seed. My father sent my mama and his two prior wives to their deaths attempting to sire an heir. I vowed not to repeat my father's mistakes. I promised myself never to marry, and I'd let the title pass to some distant cousin. I won't be the one responsible for your death."

She stepped closer, wrapped her arms about his neck, and brought his head down until their foreheads touched. "For such an intelligent man, you can be an utter dunderhead. I have no intentions of meeting my maker anytime soon, and child-birthing techniques have greatly improved in recent years."

Her touch was a soothing balm, but he needed to make her understand he could not marry. "Minerva, I can't give you the life you want most. And while I'm greedy and selfish most of the time, I love you too much to deny you the chance to be a mother."

Her gaze bored into him. "I can see you have given the subject much consideration."

The flecks of gold in her hazel eyes sent sparks of desire through him. He could only hope to contain them, like he had in the past. Although each moment that passed in her chambers was proving to be a torturous test of his will.

She kneaded the tense muscles at the back of his neck. "Let me guess…you are of the belief that if you were to win our chess match, you would be sentencing me to either a barren marriage or one that would result in my death. And…you suppose if I were to win, you will be forced to watch the woman you love marry another—is that correct?"

Simultaneously a wave of relief rolled though him and a lump formed in his throat. Wordlessly, he nodded. Why hadn't he been able to formulate such a concise and eloquent explanation? Thank goodness the woman understood him. His throat muscles relaxed.

"Now you understand why I couldn't challenge you all these years and why the outcome of our match will end in disaster," he said.

She shook her head and rolled up onto her toes. Before he knew what she was about, she pressed her lips to his, and he groaned as he gave in to temptation and kissed Minerva with abandon.

Heaving for a breath, she pulled back and said, "You are not the only one who has grievances over the outcome of our match." She slid her hands down to rest her palms against his chest.

Even though she remained physically touching him, a heaviness filled the space between their bodies. An ominous weight fell upon his shoulders. Whatever she was about to say, he didn't want to hear it.

Minerva sighed and, in a rush, said, "If I win, I shall never be able to share my love for you, and if you win I shall have to forgo an adventure of a lifetime that has taken me years to plan."

His heart swelled. He had suspected for years she held more than a sisterly affection for him, but to hear her speak of loving him bolstered his spirits, shattering his fears.

Until the second half of her sentence registered. What plans? What adventure was so important to her that she would forgo love?

He bent until their foreheads touched once more. "What a conundrum we find ourselves in."

"I agree. What do you suppose we should do?"

"We play the game, to the best of our abilities. We each should play to win."

She stepped back. "Very well. May the best player win."

He searched her features for a clue as to her true opinion on how to move forward, but her clear gaze confirmed for him that neither of them would ever be happy unless they both played for victory.

Conflicted, he reached for the door handle. "I shall eagerly await your next move."

He slipped out into the hallway and saw himself out, pausing briefly outside Kent's old rooms. His best friend would have called him out to duel if he had caught Anthony alone in Minerva's rooms.

No. Kent wasn't the violent sort—he'd have marched Anthony straight to the Doctors' Commons to seek out an application for a special license. Damn.

The probability of his marrying Minerva and denying her a future filled with a parcel of children was increasing with each passing moment. Rather than dread filling his bones, an inkling of hope sparked. A spark that was doused with doubts about his ability to give her a life of happiness. He kept to the shadows as he exited the Malbury townhouse.

Minerva had mentioned an adventure. If he could discover what the escapade entailed, he could see to it that she got to experience it after they married. For there was no way he was going to lose their match.

CHAPTER EIGHT

SEATED AT THE elegantly adorned Avondale dining table, Minerva let her gaze fell upon her plate. Being present and not letting her mind wander had always been a struggle for Minerva, and tonight was no exception. Anthony's logic for not wishing to marry her plagued her every waking moment. He claimed to be in love her but was certain childbirth would be her demise.

Would she be happy in a childless marriage?

She had never questioned the presumption that a wife to a peer should birth the next heir. Oh, the pressure to do so had been mentioned many a time behind a fluttering fan, but the question of fertility had never crossed Minerva's mind. Having pulled out her copy of *Debrett's*, Minerva could not fault Anthony in his perspective, even if his logic was not scientifically sound.

The dark form next to her shifted. Lord Camdon—a full head and a half taller than she, dark-haired, with piercing brown eyes that contained flecks of gold—was the exact opposite of Anthony, who had striking blue eyes and sandy blond hair, and was a mere half a head or so taller. The man's gaze slid to the terrace doors. Minerva peered out through the glass planes into the dark and caught something or someone move along the hedge.

Lord Camdon chuckled. "Who do you think is daft enough to attempt to spy on Avondale?"

The rich, gravelly sound put Minerva at ease. "What makes you believe they are spying? Perhaps it's simply the gardener."

"At this hour?" The lopsided grin Lord Camdon shot her way told her that this man was no stranger to flirting or gaining his way with a well-timed smile.

Curious as to what type of man she was to dine with, Minerva asked, "Should we alert our host?"

"No. I shall investigate."

Ah. A man of action. Oddly, his response pleased her more than it should, given he was a complete stranger. "I shall join you."

Mid-turn, Lord Camdon's entire body stiffened. "Does your declaration to only marry a gentleman who can defeat you at chess exempt you from scandal?"

Minerva blinked up at the man. "No."

"Then I suggest you remain here." His gaze raked over her from head to toe. "Or you shall find yourself married to me."

How presumptuous. How bold. How dare he.

Nerves rattled, she replied, "Doubtful; we are amongst family and friends. No one would—"

He grinned and interrupted her. "Do your eyes always shine bright green when you are challenged? They are extremely arresting." He held out his arm and waited for her to loop hers through it. "I'm rather tempted to take Avondale's advice and see just how well I would fare sitting across a chessboard from you."

"It's no wonder you survived abroad. Skilled at flattery, easy on the eyes, and the intelligence to gauge just how much information is needed to gain the trust of a stranger. Such skills would ensure your safety and cement your belief that no one could charm a lady better than you." She linked her arm through his. "However, it will require more than an alluring smile and a few enchanting words to gain my attention, and significantly more to defeat me at a game I've played since I broke free of my leading strings."

"My...you are magnificent. Bold. Daring. Unafraid." He

escorted her closer to the terrace doors. "It's a shame you are already in love with another, or I would be tempted to give Kent a reason to meet me at dawn once we cross the threshold."

She searched his features. Unalarmed by his serious glare, Minerva spoke loud enough for others to hear. "I'd be delighted to take a turn about the gardens." In a low, hushed whisper, she asked, "What gave you the preposterous idea that I'm in love?"

"I've been trained by England's best to read and interpret people's reactions. Was I wrong—is your heart free to love another?"

As Minerva, she was a terrible liar. Calling upon her alter ego, Madame Rose, she tilted her head, peered up, and fluttered her eyes at the man. "As shocking as this might be to you—you are wrong."

He grinned and patted her hand resting on his arm. "I don't believe I've misread you, my lady. However, I'll acknowledge you are an extremely talented actress, and it is no wonder that the Head of the Foreign Office has a keen interest in you."

Her footsteps faltered as they crossed the threshold into the dimly lit terrace. She snuck another glance up at Lord Camdon. Bah. The man didn't know of her secret identity. He was fishing for information. The gold flecks in his gaze sparkled with interest, not confidence.

Lord Camdon's gaze was solely trained upon her, but his muscles beneath her palm tensed for a blink of an eye. She scanned the perimeter. Anthony was close by. She couldn't see him, but her heart was racing.

Her companion released a sigh, one that was tinged with frustration. Lord Camdon stopped and bent to whisper in her ear, "If there was someone out here, they've since left."

She stepped in front of him and stretched up to snake her arms about his neck. "I believe you are wrong again, my lord."

With confidence and ease, Lord Camdon wrapped his arms about her waist, and she waited—hoped—Anthony would make himself known. Her logic was sound. Anthony had shared with her that he loved her. He claimed he couldn't bear to see another man marry her.

Then why was the blasted man not coming forth?

Lord Camdon tilted his head, and his warm breath ran down her neck as he whispered, "You are playing a dangerous game, Lady Minerva. Agents are trained to never let their feelings interfere. Drake is a natural; he is renowned for his ability to rein in his emotions and act with ice in his veins."

"You've known all this time Drake was here?"

"No. But you…you can sense him. Your muscles are wound tight." He rubbed his thumb along the base of her spine.

His bold touches weren't offensive, but were of a brotherly nature, comforting and reassuring, as opposed to the sparks Anthony ignited within her with a mere look.

She rolled back down to firmly plant her feet on the ground. Her hands skimmed over his lapel. "Thank you, my lord, for being honest with me. And for providing insight into the mind of an agent. Or in this case, a mere gentleman."

"Drake is no ordinary gentleman. We both know that to be a fact." Lord Camdon had spoken loud enough that if Anthony was near, as she suspected, he would have heard. Slowly removing his arms from about her waist, Lord Camdon wound them firmly behind his back, his gaze never leaving her face. He was keenly observing her every reaction. "Lady Minerva, it would be an honor if you would agree to play a game of chess with me."

The man's features were in the shadows and hard to read. Why would Lord Camdon issue the challenge? Why now? Had Anthony overheard?

She stared back at the man that was calmly awaiting her reply. He was an official agent of the Foreign Office. A spy. Purported to be a very talented and dutiful member of the agency. Loyal. Devoted. Which meant he would marry if ordered to.

Minerva peered up and asked, "Did the Head of the Foreign Office order you to challenge me, in order to recruit me?"

"Regardless of whether or not I was ordered to issue the challenge, I sincerely hope you will accept."

Ha. She would wager a month's worth of pin money she was correct. "If I didn't know better, I'd have guessed that the Head of the Foreign Office was some old, matchmaking biddy. What I don't understand is why your leader, who has the weighty responsibility for our country's international relations, would go to such extremes to recruit me. He is a rather tenacious fellow."

The corner of Lord Camdon's lips twitched at her last statement. Odd. Her brother-in-law-to-be had had a similar reaction when she referred to the agency's leader as being male. Could the Head of the Foreign Office be, in fact, a woman?

Intrigued by the notion, Minerva's mind wandered once more. Having spent time with Avondale, it was clear to her that whoever the leader of the Foreign Office was, they were well respected, and their unorthodox methods were revered.

"Lady Minerva..." Lord Camdon had clearly recognized that her thoughts drifted. "Shall we play a game of chess?"

"Only if you and the Head of the Foreign Office agree to my terms..." Terms that she quickly formulated and assessed for viability.

"And what are these conditions you insist upon?"

"If I win, your leader will cease to harass me into joining your ranks. If you win, we shall marry—however, only if that is your wish, not your leader's."

"Very well. I shall share your terms with my leader and inform you of their decision on the morrow."

Lord Camdon had once again deftly avoided using gender-specific pronouns. Now that she pondered on it, no one referred to the Head of the Foreign Office as "he." All these years she had assumed it was a gentleman. It would be mad to think that the king would allow a woman to govern over such a critical department for the country. Ah, but the king was unconventional, to put it mildly.

The tinkle of the dinner bell broke her train of thought. Lord

Camdon offered his arm, and she noted the back of her neck no longer tingled. Anthony must have left at some point during their conversation. How peculiar—normally so in tune was she with Anthony that she should have noticed.

As she approached the terrace doors, guests were lining up to leave to go to the dining room. She searched for her sisters, but neither Isadora nor Diana were in sight, reminding her that they had moved on. Diana was happily married to Chestwick, and Isadora was soon be wed. It was what Minerva had planned. It was what she'd wished for. Yet the joy of a successfully executed plan was distinctly missing.

Lord Camdon led her through the doors. "If I convince my superior to agree to your terms, would you entertain the idea of the match being conducted at my residence…properly chaperoned, of course?"

"Why your residence?"

"I'd like for you to become familiar with your new home."

The man's ego wasn't lacking by any means. His self-assuredness made her smile. "You are rather confident of your chess skills."

Lord Camdon winked. "That, or perhaps I have faith in my skills of persuasion."

His reply made her chuckle. "If your leader agrees to my terms, then it will be Kent whom you will be persuading to allow our game to take place in your home. My brother oversees all my chess matches."

All but one. Minerva had skillfully avoided her brother since the night he visited her bedchambers. Benedict would not be happy to discover she was traipsing to the outskirts of Mayfair to play Anthony in private.

"Hm. I wonder who it will take more exception to the location—your brother or Drake?" Lord Camdon waggled his eyebrows at her. Bother. The man was clearly skilled at reading a person. She'd have to be careful if they were indeed to sit across from one another in front of a chessboard.

ANTHONY RAKED A hand through his hair to dislodge the prickly leaves. He should have returned to his lodgings when Camdon and Minerva spotted him in the hedges and came out to investigate. Combined, the two were exceptionally hard to evade, and he had shifted further out of sight and hearing than what he had wished to. They didn't pursue him, but rather engaged in what appeared to be an intimate conversation that had Minerva behaving in a way he'd never witnessed before with a gentleman. Oh, the woman had flirted with others in the past, but always at a distance.

He had learned how to control his jealousy to rein in his need to claim her as his. But tonight, rage roared through his veins as Camdon dared to hold Minerva close. It wasn't in Anthony's nature to act before assessing all the various aspects of a situation. So as he stalked the pair back to the house, he was forced to analyze the facts. The truth was that Camdon was a good fellow. Intelligent. Trustworthy. Came from a large brood of healthy males. He would make Minerva a fine husband.

To hell with logic. Minerva was his.

With his stomach in knots, he crouched and waited for the couple to reenter. As they shifted out of sight, Anthony moved along the wall to peer through the dining room window. Damn. Minerva's back was to him, and she was seated opposite Camdon, an agent who was renowned for disguising his true thoughts. He wouldn't be able to trust Camdon's facial expressions, nor read his lips. His once boon companion was extremely adept at deception.

Minerva's shoulders bobbed up and down slightly as if she was laughing. Camdon was most likely charming her with stories of his travels. Her adventurous spirit would be enthralled by such tales.

Anthony's chest ached, along with his stomach. He was in

agony. He slumped to lean against the stone wall. He'd never ventured farther than to his Scottish estate, and that was a rare occurrence.

He rose to peer at the evening affair that he would have surely been invited to if he were not in hiding. Avondale, host and one of the more reserved agents for the Foreign Office, sat staring at his fiancée Isadora with calm eyes. Then there was Chestwick, who smiled at his wife Diana as if sharing a private moment. The war hero no longer shielded others from the ghastly gash that ran along the left side of his face.

Egad. Was that what marriage did to a man? Transformed him into a better version of himself?

The candlelight flickered and drew Anthony's attention back to Camdon, whose gaze narrowed and focused upon the window ledge. Anthony sank to his bottom as Minerva turned to peer over her shoulder. He had imagined it would be difficult to witness Minerva being courted by another, but to also be excluded from his friends was pure torture.

For years, this was what he'd wished for Minerva: to find a gentleman who could give her the life she'd always dreamt of. He should be happy for her. Camdon could give her what he couldn't.

The stabbing pain in his chest called him out. He didn't truly want Minerva to marry another.

A ghostly white image of Minerva flashed before his mind's eye. She would die if she married him.

He scrambled along the wall, and as soon as he was at the building's edge, he got to his feet and ran. Ran into the darkness. Every stratagem and plan he'd ever considered whirled through his mind as he pumped his arms and legs.

He needed Minerva. There had to be an alternative to her death or unhappiness if they were to marry. Why were his thoughts always so clouded when it came to her?

He pushed himself to go faster, harder, until he was gasping for air. Hands on his knees, he looked up to find himself in front of the Malbury townhouse.

He couldn't risk entering.

He shouldn't wait for Minerva to return. And yet he wasn't ready to return to his empty lodgings across Town.

As unwise as it was, he proceeded to sneak into the Malbury residence and headed directly for Minerva's chambers.

CHAPTER NINE

"Y OU'VE BEEN RATHER quiet all night." Isadora's green eyes narrowed upon Minerva in the dimly lit coach as they returned from Avondale's mansion.

"Have I?" Minerva's thoughts had continued to circle throughout the evening, always returning to her game with Anthony. Anxiety over her next move, which could very well determine whether she won or lost, had preoccupied her mentally for most of the evening, despite Lord Camdon's attempts to charm her.

"You have, and you know it. Are you worried about Drake and his sudden disappearance?" Her sister patted her knee like Minerva used to do to ease Isadora's nerves when they were younger. Isadora didn't care for physical affection, still didn't, but she did allow family to breach the distinct personal barrier she preferred to maintain. "Avondale says there is naught to worry about. Hm…" Her brow wrinkled. "Although, come to think upon it, my dear fiancé was rather vague about his whereabouts and employed his devious skills to distract me." Color flooded her cheeks.

Isadora was engaged to Avondale, to be married in two weeks, and Minerva could very well guess what tactics her future brother-in-law had employed. She gave Isadora a side glance. It was all that was needed to put an end to their conversation.

The coach rattled steadily along until they arrived back in front of Malbury Townhouse. Minerva peered out the coach window and let out a deep sigh. The structure that was once occupied by all of her family now appeared cold and empty. Her father rarely spent more than the occasional evening in the master chambers. Her mama spent the majority of her evenings away and slept most of the day. With Paul away at school, and Benedict and Diana married, that left Gregory, Isadora, and her in the house. But Gregory spent his evenings attending the hospital, and Isadora would soon be married too.

The coach door flung open, and Minerva forced herself to exit.

With a slight bounce in her step, Isadora swooshed by. "Time for sleep, sister. Tomorrow shall be another full day of planning and packing."

Malbury Townhouse would be lonely without her sisters. Minerva stood at the foot of the path that led to the front door and looked up to the window of her chambers. The curtains fluttered. Someone was in her rooms.

Anthony.

Skirts clutched tightly in her hands, Minerva attempted to remain calm and moderated her steps. She should be furious at the man for daring to invade her space knowing she wasn't home. Yet excitement built within her as she took each step, bringing her closer to Anthony.

The complexity of the outcomes of their game weighed heavily on her shoulders all day and eve. With no one to discuss the details with, Minerva was eager to see Anthony.

Her steps slowed as she recognized the truth—Anthony was no unbiased party. His analytical skills, which had proven valuable over the years, would be swayed by his own hopes and wishes, clouding his judgment just as her dreams were muddling her own conclusions.

She trudged up the stairs. Her longstanding debate over the advantages and disadvantages of becoming Madame Rose remained unresolved. She acknowledged that, as selfish as it was, her desire to be free, to be someone else—someone the complete opposite of what the *ton* expected of her as Lady Minerva Malbury—held an allure that rivaled her deep-seated love for Anthony.

She marched down the hall past the portrait of her ancestors who would shake their heads at her if they could. Minerva mumbled, "I know I have no one to blame but myself for this predicament."

She reached her chamber and pushed open the door that was slightly ajar. Barnett, her maid, was turning down the sheets. "Oh, beg pardon, my lady. There was a commotion earlier in the kitchens that delayed me. I'll have your bed ready—"

"Nothing to fret about, Barnett. I'm in no rush." Minerva scanned her room. Where was Anthony hiding?

Barnett gave a pillow one more quick fluff and then moved to assist her to undress. Minerva stood stock-still. She wouldn't be able to get out of her gown unassisted.

A tingling sensation ran down her arms all the way to her fingertips. The thought of Drake watching her undress both unnerved and excited her.

Her maid made quick work of the row of buttons, and moments later Minerva stood clad only in a slip. "My thanks, Barnett. I think I shall stay up and read for a bit."

"Shall I fetch you extra candles?"

"Not tonight."

Barnett picked up Minerva's discarded gown and stays, bobbed, and left the room.

She waited for the door to close. "You can come out now."

Anthony rolled out from under her bed and tugged at the hem of his jacket. "How did you know I was here?"

"Besides my catching you spying out of my window from down below, the skin on the back of my neck prickles every time you are close, regardless of if you are in my line of sight or not. In addition, there is that faint scent of sandalwood that unmistakably belongs to you."

"I smell lemons when you are near." He came to stand before her.

She had begun bathing with lemon soap the day he shared it was his favorite scent. At first, she had hoped the scent would entice him to remain close to her. That theorem quickly proved to be faulty. Then, over time, the fresh citrus scent became calming, and she couldn't fathom having a different scent upon her skin. Many of her habits originated from a desire to capture Anthony's attention but grew to become simply part of who she was.

She placed her hands on her hips and tilted her chin up to ask, "Why were you skulking about in Avondale's gardens tonight?"

"Because I needed...I wanted to speak with you." Drake ran the back of his knuckles along her jaw. "Seeing you tonight at Avondale's without me, I realize how stupid I've been all these years. I love you, and I intend to win our match."

He had confessed to loving her the other night, but hearing it again solidified her confusion. "I don't understand. Why the change of heart? Why do you wish to marry me? Why now? What of your fear of killing me?" She stopped her queries to take a breath. She had barely begun to share the long list of questions that she wished for answers to.

Anthony reached for her right hand and held it between both of his warm, gloved hands. "That is what I needed to speak to you about. I've come here to ask...could you be happy loving me and me alone for the rest of our days?"

A high-pitched ringing tone echoed in her ears. She blinked and refocused on Anthony, who was squeezing her hand. "Are you asking me if I would be willing to forgo the opportunity of children?"

"Yes, exactly."

It had taken only a few discreet inquires, and Minerva had learned that Anthony's fears of death by childbirth were valid— while not as common as it once was, there remained a high mortality rate, meriting his concern. After her discovery, she'd attempted to picture a future with Anthony sans children. The joy she experienced fantasizing of a life together with him hadn't faded, and wasn't impacted by the possibility of never having children. Children didn't foster love between parents. Her and her siblings' existence had proven that. It was Minerva's belief that her father loved her mother less with each child she'd birthed.

Children or no children, she loved Anthony. But loving the man didn't preclude her from wanting the adventure she had spent three long Seasons devising.

Minerva pulled her hand from his and searched his features. The lines at the corners of his eyes indicated worry, but his gaze also held a hint of anger. "Your sudden change of heart...it has nothing to do with Lord Camdon?"

"I'd be lying if I said that seeing you in another man's arms this eve had been a pleasant experience." He stepped back two paces. "Do you find yourself attracted to Lord Camdon?"

Anthony *had* been jealous. He'd stated he loved her, twice. He'd claimed he wanted to win their match and marry her. It was what she had wanted for so long, yet now he had said it, why wasn't she over-the-moon excited?

"You should know that Lord Camdon has challenged me to a chess match."

"Did you accept the challenge?"

"Yes and no." She turned and paced the length of her bed. She needed to sort through all the rioting thoughts and emotions. As she passed by him, she explained, "I agreed to play dependent on certain terms. Specifically, if I were to win, the Head of the Foreign Office would cease their attempts to recruit me."

Anthony's jaw dropped for a moment, and then he asked, "Camdon was ordered to challenge you?"

Minerva stopped and faced him. "Yes, much like yourself."

"But I love you."

"And I've told you, I love you too. But that doesn't change

the situation. The Head of the Foreign Office has decided it's their right to intervene. By demanding they cease and desist from any further matchmaking schemes, it is the only way I can ensure I'm free to choose my own future."

Anthony stepped closer. "And that is what you truly wish for…the ability to choose."

"Yes."

"You do not fear Camdon might defeat you?"

She pondered over her interactions with Lord Camdon. The man would be a worthy opponent. However, she was certain the gentleman's arrogance would ensure his defeat. "No, I do not. Do you think Lord Camdon has the ability to defeat me?"

"I haven't been in the man's company for many years. If he remains as sharp as I remember, he will not be easily defeated."

Anthony's assessment gave her pause. To date, his judgment of others had proven to be acutely accurate, and if Anthony believed it possible for her to lose, she'd have to ensure she employed a sound strategy to defeat Lord Camdon. "I shan't worry about that until I hear whether or not the Head of the Foreign Office agrees to my terms. My current concern is the outcome of *our* chess match."

He arched a brow at her. "Afraid you might lose?"

"Yes." She swallowed hard as she added, "And…I'm also afraid I might win."

He bent a little lower until they were eye to eye. "You won't win."

Annoyance bubbled up within her. Damn the man's green eyes, full of confidence and…and that twinkle that made her insides and mind turn to mushed turnips. His cocky reply should make her want to turn him away, except it had the opposite effect. She loved it when he challenged her versus acceding to her.

She crossed her arms over her chest. "We shall have to see about that."

His gaze flickered to the tops of her breasts. Ha. She was able to tempt the man. For years he'd given her no clue as to if he returned her regard, leaving her hopeless. Whatever barricade he'd built to shield his thoughts and feelings was slowly crumbling, and she wasn't certain if she should be elated or livid at the change. She was certainly cautious not to reveal her confusion.

"I'm an idiot for not challenging you in your first Season," he said. "I'm a fool for not doing so in your second or third Season, but trust me when I say I've come to my senses."

His response doused any sparks of anger within her. "You are a dullard for assuming I wanted a large family. You never asked what I really wanted."

He hung his head. "Tell me, then, what is it that you really want?"

Minerva wrapped her arms around his waist and pressed her cheek to his chest. "If you had asked me a year ago, I would have said you."

Chin on top of her head, he asked, "And now?"

"Now? Now I'm not certain."

He wrapped her in his arms and hugged her close. "I'm sorry for mucking everything up."

A sense of security and well-being enveloped her. If she were to lose to Anthony, he would without a doubt love and care for her, but she would never know what it would be like to live as Madame Rose—free and independent.

"Will you send word if you are to play Camdon?"

"I shall. And if I'm to play Lord Camdon, I suggest we adjust the terms of our match—we lift the restriction of one play per person per day."

He pulled back to search her eyes. "I agree, if you allow me a kiss."

The glint in Anthony's gaze left no doubt in Minerva's mind that the man had no intention of letting her win. His request was a reminder of what she would be sacrificing. If she wanted to taste what life could be like as an indepedent woman, she'd have to win and forgo marriage to this man—and his kisses.

She rolled up onto the balls of her feet and pressed her lips to his. He clutched her to him. Every inch of her was pressed against his hard body. She wanted to melt into him. Shock waves of pleasure rolled down her back as his tongue grazed her bottom lip. Never kissing Anthony again would be a hefty price to pay for independence.

He broke off the kiss and bent to carry her to bed. Her mind raced with possibilities. Would he lie with her? Would he take the decision of marriage entirely out of her hands?

She needn't have worried, for as soon as her bottom touched the bed, he tucked her in like a child and left, practically running from the room.

Typical Anthony. Always leaving her wondering.

CHAPTER TEN

BODY AND MIND fatigued, Minerva forced herself to take one step after another walking about in a circle in front of the drawing room window, only stopping periodically to scan the busy road. Three hours of sleep was insufficient, but it was all her mind had allowed as the list of concerns surrounding her immediate future mounted with each passing hour. If she continued to pace about, she wouldn't have to address the litany of questions posed by her younger sisters which had begun as soon as she set foot into the drawing room. She'd never had an issue with providing a satisfactory answer or solution that would ease her sisters' worries in the past—however, for the first time, Minerva was at a total loss as to respond.

Arms crossed over her chest, Isadora stood next to the fireplace, gaze trained on the flames. "Given that I'm to marry Avondale, and we are to journey to Spain after we are wed…what could be so pressing that the Head of the Foreign Office would go to such great lengths to recruit Minerva?"

"A threat to the Crown for certain." Diana leaned her head back against the back of the settee and closed her eyes.

Minerva's heart ached—apparently, she wasn't the only one not getting enough rest. She pressed her fingers to her temples to ease the tension that was mounting. Minerva had considered a myriad of scenarios in an attempt to determine why, after all these years of passive invitations and polite denials, the Head of the Foreign Office was determined to recruit her into the agency.

"Sister." Isadora crossed the room to join her in front of the window, blocking the dim rays of sunlight. "If your head is aching, why don't you go lie down? I promise to send for you should we receive word from Lord Camdon."

Minerva shook her head.

Diana rose also and joined them by the window. "If you are to play Lord Camdon, you shall need your wits about you. That is, if you wish to win. Or perhaps you found him intriguing enough to consider marriage."

Minerva's gaze switched from one sister to the other. How had the roles been reversed? Her sisters were the ones ordering her about her instead of the other way around.

The pounding in her head increased, and she resigned herself to the fact that Diana was right: her brain needed more rest. Especially if she were required to play two games this eve, one with Lord Camdon and the continuation of her match with Anthony. Without a clear head, she would be placing her future in jeopardy.

"While I found Lord Camdon to be rather clever and pleasant company, I don't believe we would suit. He's far more of a traditionalist than what he lets on. If I'm to marry, I wish for a gentleman who possesses an open mind and an engaged heart." She gave her sisters a smile and continued, "A brief respite in my chambers does sound like a wonderful idea."

Engulfed in a hug from both her sisters, Minerva enjoyed the moment. With Isadora marrying a spy, and Diana and Chestwick's preference for the countryside, it would be a rare occurrence for the three of them to be together, and in private.

As she expected, Isadora was the first to release her, and then, with one last squeeze, Diana too stepped back and let Minerva go.

"Go rest, sister. Avondale is quite adamant that if you were to play Lord Camdon, it will be no easy feat." Isadora turned her by the shoulders to face the door.

Minerva left the drawing room and trudged up the stairs. What if Lord Camdon proved to be as astute as Avondale claimed? She was skilled in strategy, but knowing her opponent—their motives, strengths, and weaknesses—was what aided her in developing a winning strategy even before they sat down to play. She knew little of Lord Camdon. From their brief acquaintance, she'd deduced he was a man not easily deterred once his mind was set. He'd also made it clear to her that he wasn't looking for a love match but a wife with whom he could converse and discuss weightier topics than the weather.

She paused outside her chamber door. Sandalwood. Anthony had left hours ago; there was no reason his scent should linger. He wouldn't have dared to return so soon, not in broad day-light—or would he?

Minerva pushed open the door. Half of her wanted to see the man who made her pulse accelerate, and the other half wanted to avoid discussing the future with Anthony.

Eyes closed, Anthony lay upon her bed with his hands cra-dling the back of his head. He didn't move, nor utter a sound.

She crept closer until she stood next to him.

"You will have to teach me how to move soundlessly." An-thony opened his eyes and grinned. "Are you to play Camdon?"

Argh. The man was infuriatingly jovial, and up close she could see he was well rested. No dark circles under Anthony's eyes, unlike the black smudges she had. "I told you last eve I'd alert you as soon as I received word. Do you not trust me to do as I say?"

"I do." He wiggled to the middle of the bed and patted the space he had just vacated.

She resisted the invisible tug to join him and planted her hands on her hips. The gall of the man, inviting her to lie next to him in her own bed. "Why are you really here?"

"I'm—"

His sheepish look said it all, and she answered her own question. "You're lonely." Despite her better judgment, she slipped onto the bed and sat next to him, resting her back against the headboard. "If I were you, I'd be taking advantage of this opportunity to face your demons."

His whole body tensed. "What do you know of my anxieties?"

She slid down the bed and rolled to face him. "I know everything about you."

"And you are still willing to marry me?"

"If I lose our game, yes."

Anthony rolled onto his side to mirror her position. His gaze locked on her, and she forgot all about their game, about Lord Camdon, about her dreams of being Madame Rose for a Season...she forgot about everything and concentrated on the simple task of breathing.

On a whispered breath, Anthony said, "I see."

What did he see? Did he understand her confusion?

He cupped the side of her face. The pad of his thumb circled her temple. "You have no intentions of losing, do you?" He leaned in closer, closed his eyes, and pressed his forehead to hers. It was as if he was trying to read her mind. "If you win, I shall leave you alone, and I promise not to interfere with your plans." Anthony dragged in a deep breath. "However, I fully intend to win, and I promise you...marriage to me shall be far more rewarding than any adventure you may have planned."

Drugged by his touch, she remained quiet and let his words filter through her mind. Anthony rarely made promises. For him to make two in succession meant he was not taking matters lightly.

He pulled back from her. "Rest. I'll wait for you across Town to continue our game. If you are to play Camdon...we can delay our game, if that is what you wish."

She didn't know what she wanted.

"You don't have to decide now—wait until you hear from Camdon."

Minerva nodded. She closed her eyes as he pressed a chaste kiss to her forehead and rolled off the bed.

When she opened her eyes, he was gone. He could move soundlessly. He didn't need her to help to master the skill.

Minerva rolled onto her back and inhaled. Anthony's scent filled her lungs. A warm sensation settled over her. It was like he was still there lying next to her. The tension in her neck and temples eased.

Eyes closed, she let her mind drift back to memories of when Anthony first came to Malbury Mansion, accompanying Benedict home for the holidays. After that, Anthony never failed to appear on their doorstep to spend school break with them. She was so eager to see him, to spend time with him, she'd never questioned why Anthony spent every holiday with them instead of his own family. If she lost, nothing would change; if she won, he'd never spend another holiday with her again.

A heaviness filled her heart. Why was giving up her dream of becoming Madame Rose for a Season so difficult?

THE PATTER OF slippers moving hurriedly about woke Minerva from a deep slumber. She peered through her eyelids to find both Diana and Isadora pacing about her room. She rolled up to sit and rubbed her eyes. "How long have I been asleep?"

"Not long. An hour at most." Isadora wrung her hands. "Lord Camdon has arrived."

"And?"

Diana marched over to the bed. "The Head of the Foreign Office has agreed to your terms. You are to play Lord Camdon."

Worry marred both her sisters' foreheads. The pair were not faint of heart. Minerva stood and shook out her skirts, granting her the extra moment she needed to compose herself. "Do you question my ability to win?"

Diana, who stood next to her, answered. "Chestwick and Avondale have been discussing strategy. Chestwick believes Camdon can be defeated, but Avondale is not so certain. Our dear future brother-in-law's doubt is probably due to the fact that he has yet to witness your brilliance when playing chess."

"My fiancé is well aware of Minerva's abilities," Isadora said. "He may not have firsthand experience like Chestwick, but Minerva's skill and gameplay is widely known. Avondale's opinion is valid."

Minerva shook her head. "I didn't ask what Avondale or Chestwick's opinion was. I asked whether or not you believed Lord Camdon capable of defeating me." She walked over to her washstand, poured water into the porcelain basin, and proceeded to splash cold water on her face. Fully awake, Minerva patted her face dry and turned to face her sisters. "Well?"

Diana shrugged. "We know little of Lord Camdon's motives, nor are we familiar with the gentleman's strengths and weaknesses."

Isadora chimed in, "Plus we know nothing of how his mind operates, except that he is extremely well regarded by both his superiors and his peers."

Her sisters' concerns echoed her earlier thoughts: Lord Camdon was an unknown. A stranger. Outliers had a propensity to have luck on their side, but Minerva preferred to rely on skill than a stroke of good fortune. "Where is the match to be conducted?"

"We are to attend the Harmon Ball, as planned," Isadora replied. "Lord Camdon will be present, and he will publicly issue his challenge. Avondale confirmed Lady Harmon has already been informed of tonight's entertainment."

"Then there is no time to waste. Let's invite our dear Lord Camdon for tea and discover as much as possible."

Minerva started for the door. From behind, Diana said, "We already sent for Lord Camdon. He should have arrived. Avondale and Chestwick were instructed to entertain him until we came down."

A burst of pride at her sisters' actions filled Minerva's heart. She stopped and turned to face her youngest sister.

Before she could praise Diana, her younger sister placed a hand on her arm and glanced at Isadora before whispering, "Chestwick shared with me that spies are notorious for lying and are masters of deceit."

Isadora marched up to Diana. "Are you calling your future brother-in-law, my husband-to-be, a liar?"

"I am. While I'm fully aware it's all for the greater good, Minerva needs to be on her guard. It is highly unlikely Camdon will reveal his true intentions."

Marriage suited Minerva's youngest sister, as it would Isadora, but what of her?

"The both of you stop fretting and have faith that I shall prevail." Minerva squared her shoulders and mentally donned an invisible suit of armor, prepared to go into battle with an unfamiliar opponent.

As they descended the stairs, a wave of male laughter halted Minerva mid-step. She had always hoped her sisters' husbands and her own would merely become an extension of their close family. Chestwick's deep tones, mixed with that of Isadora's Avondale, harmonized with Lord Camdon and her brother Gregory's laughter.

Minerva's chest tightened. Her family had been her priority for so long—would she be able to live as Madame Rose, on the outer fringes of society, not able to interact daily with her siblings? But wasn't that the point of her plan—to seize one Season for herself? To do as she wished without the restraints of being a lady, the daughter of a viscount?

"Minerva, is something amiss?" Isadora asked.

Minerva glanced over her shoulder at her sisters. Both wore a glow of happiness. They were all grown and no longer in need of her guidance. "No. I was attempting to decipher the cause for the gentlemen's gaiety."

Isadora grinned. "I heard Gregory's laughter amongst them, which leads me to believe he's home for an impromptu visit and probably regaling them with one of his bawdy stories from university."

Minerva picked up her skirts and continued her descent. She would miss her brother's unpredictable visits. Paul, her youngest brother, turned eighteen in a month. Would he forgive her for missing his birthday?

Weaknesses in what she had previously believed to be a solid plan were starting to emerge. Self-doubt that she normally managed to ignore was now roaring in her ears.

What if she lost to Lord Camdon this eve?

Not only would she not marry the man she'd loved all her life, she would also be forced to give up all plans of becoming Madame Rose.

Losing to Lord Camdon was not an option. In order to win, she needed information.

She marched into the drawing room, set to disarm Lord Camdon and discover the man's weaknesses. Except she stopped short a mere three steps past the threshold at the sight of the men relaxed, all conversing with one another. It was a picture of perfect harmony. A camaraderie that only ever existed in her fanciful fantasies of a joyful future with her siblings and their spouses.

Diana and Isadora continued into the room, and Minerva noted the broad, happy smiles of her sisters as they made their way to sit upon the settee. While her sisters chose to be seated the socially required distance from their mates, the invisible bonds that tied them to the men they had chosen to spend the rest of their lives with were clearly visible to Minerva.

The gentlemen rose, breaking her train of thought and prompting her to take another step forward. Lord Camdon met her halfway. "A pleasure to see you again, Lady Minerva. May I have a word with you…in private?"

She bobbed a quick curtsy and answered, "Shall we take a

turn about the room? Or would you prefer outdoors?"

"Outdoors—however, I believe it more prudent if we remain in sight of the others." He held out his arm for her, and as soon as her arm looped through his, he began to escort her about the perimeter of the room. "Did your sisters inform you of the Head of the Foreign Office's decision?"

"Yes, they did. However, I must share I'm rather surprised."

Lord Camdon chuckled. "I'm not. My superior is extremely fair and reasonable."

Her opponent appeared to be in rather fine spirits, not at all worried about their pending match. She peered up and asked, "Will you join us for tea?"

"And give away all my secrets? I think not." Lord Camdon gave her a smile. "The truth is, I can't stay. I must see to a certain matter prior to our engagement later this evening."

The tinge of frustration in his last statement prompted Minerva to ask, "What exactly did you have to agree to in order to convince your kind, dear superior to agree to my terms?"

He stared down at her with dark, serious eyes. "Nothing that I wasn't willing to do in order to gain the opportunity to seek out your hand."

Interesting. She didn't think she could be charmed by such arrogance, especially not from a stranger. Oddly, rather than raising her ire, Lord Camdon's response evoked a feeling of being singled out…chosen…sought out, which was entirely unfamiliar after years of waiting for Anthony to come to his senses. And his perspective on their match was a far cry from the views of her previous challengers, who saw her as either chattel to be won or a woman to be reined in.

Lord Camdon bowed and took his leave with long, confident strides.

A surge of exhilaration or panic, Minerva wasn't sure which, rolled through her. Avondale was correct: it would be no easy feat to claim victory over the mysterious Lord Camdon.

CHAPTER ELEVEN

U NABLE TO STAND solitary isolation any longer, Anthony left his stifling, silent townhouse and strode down the street, headed directly to seek out the help of his best friend. Kent could assist him in his investigation into Minerva's plans. He entered through the servants' door to Kent's modest lodgings that had once served as a meeting place for Cunningham, Kent, and himself.

If Anthony were to marry Minerva, that would leave Cunningham as the last to remain unwed, just as Anthony had predicted ten years ago. Cunningham would owe him a small fortune. Being the eldest of the three Cunninghams, he had wagered he'd be the first to marry. Except the man forgot to take into account his propensity to fault others, ruling out lady after lady, year after year. Cunningham's quest for the perfect lady had ensured Anthony would win their wager, although secretly, Anthony had hoped a lady would prove him wrong.

It was late afternoon. If Kent was in residence, he'd most likely be in his study. Anthony tiptoed through the halls that were peculiarly devoid of staff. Kent wasn't short of funds, so where was everyone?

He entered the room lined with reference guides and journals. Kent's study appeared abandoned. What in the blazes was going on? His best friend rarely left his study.

With the window half obstructed by a tall stack of books, Anthony proceeded to light a candle and scan the room. There was no sign of Kent, and by the thick layer of dust upon the desk, it appeared no one had entered the room for days, if not weeks.

Anthony slumped into the wing-back chair facing the window and stared out, not seeing anything or anyone. Even under Kent's roof, he was alone.

A rather large lump formed in his throat, partially blocking his airway. Memories of wandering the deathly quiet and empty halls of his country estate as a child flooded his thoughts, and a heaviness settled in his chest. The only method to prove successful in dispelling the horrid void within him was to have Minerva within sight.

Damn. What a buffoon he was to have taken her presence for granted all these years. The threat of her winning their match, not knowing where she was going or what she was doing, gave him the chills. His existence would be desolate.

Booted footsteps in the hall alerted him to Kent's arrival. He stood and turned to face the door. His best friend walked in preoccupied reading a pamphlet, probably on the latest scientific or agricultural findings.

Anthony cleared his throat. "Discover anything of interest?"

Kent lowered the paper and frowned. "Drake? What in the blazes are you doing still in Town?"

"I yielded to the Head of Foreign Office's wishes and challenged your sister to a game of chess." He waited for Kent's cheeks to redden with anger, or for his hands to clench into fists. But his best friend did neither.

Kent simply walked over to his desk and placed the parchment on top of a large stack of account ledgers. "You still have not answered my question: why are you here?"

"Minerva agreed to play me but requested we do so in private. I've been in hiding for the past few days. However, it seems the Head of the Foreign Office has no confidence in my success and sent Camdon to issue a challenge also."

"Joshua, the Earl of Camdon? Our classmate? I thought the man was still abroad on the Continent somewhere."

"He was summoned home." Anthony raked his hand through his hair. The fact that the Head of the Foreign Office was aggressively recruiting Minerva was an issue. He simply didn't have the resources or the depth of informants necessary to uncover the reasoning behind the Foreign Office's leader's actions. It was clearly apparent Minerva possessed a talent that the government official deemed highly valuable. A talent not many were aware she possessed.

On the precipice of a revelation, Anthony frowned in concentration.

Kent rounded his desk and sat. "I rather liked Camdon."

With his train of thought disrupted, Anthony refocused on the discussion at hand. "I did too, until I saw Minerva in his arms last night."

"You saw *what?*" Kent jumped up from his chair, knocking the furniture to the floor.

He was a mighty fine boxer. It probably wasn't wise to raise Kent's ire.

"Nothing scandalous occurred. Minerva knows what she's about."

Anthony moved to stand by the window and peered out. Carriages were returning from the direction of Hyde Park. Promenade hour was over.

He turned to face Kent, who remained standing, fists clenched, at the ready to hit something. "I've broken my promise to Minerva and have come out of hiding to seek out your help."

Kent glared at him. "Help you with what?"

"I must discover what Minerva has planned that is worth more to her than marrying me."

"Now that's a rather egotistical statement."

"Minerva has admitted that she loves me." Kent's frown deepened, but Anthony continued before his friend could round the desk and plant a facer. "She even confessed that, a year ago, she would have happily married me if I had challenged her and won, but that is no longer the case. She is playing to win…to go on some damn adventure. What if both Camdon and I were to lose? Don't you want to know what Minerva has planned?"

Kent spun on his heel and headed for the door.

"Where are you going?" Anthony followed Kent, hot on his heels.

"We are going to pay Aunt Adelaide a visit."

Excellent. As always, his best friend had once again come through with an actionable solution.

⊱⊰

ANTHONY STOOD IN the middle of the small but bright and cozy front room of Kent's aunt Adelaide's dwelling, which mirrored its owner's disposition.

Aunt Adelaide, who treated Anthony like a family member, waltzed into the room and immediately wrapped him in a hug. "Oh my! What a treat to have you both visit me today."

The gray-haired beauty released him and shifted to give Kent the same loving treatment, stretching her small arm around his waist.

Kent engulfed the small woman. "Aunt Adelaide, I'm pleased to see you remain hale and happy."

"Well, of course I'm happy." She released Kent and grinned up at her nephew. "Your sisters arrived in Town early, and they have been wonderful company." The small woman stepped back and motioned for them to take a seat.

Kent did as she suggested and relaxed back into the worn but clean settee. Anthony wasn't sure the petite piece of furniture would support them both, and moved to stand by the window, his preferred location in any room.

"Speaking of my dear, beloved sisters, when are you and Minerva to set off on your grand adventure across the pond?"

Aunt Adelaide's eyes momentarily went wide, and then, with a plastered smile, she slumped into the nearest chair. "Didn't Minerva inform you of our plans upon your arrival in Town?" The poor woman clasped and unclasped her hands in her lap as she braved Kent's intense stare.

"Actually, Minerva has remained rather vague regarding your voyage." Kent leaned forward, placing a hand on his knee. "I've..." Kent slid a glance over his shoulder at Anthony and then continued, "No, *we've* come today to seek your help."

"I see." Aunt Adelaide peered over at Anthony. The sweet, innocent woman was clearly befuddled. Aunt Adelaide couldn't tell a fib even if her life depended upon it. "So you've both come here today to ask me for assistance?"

It was time Anthony joined the conversation. "Aunt Adelaide, I've—"

Aunt Adelaide's eyes widened as if she'd come to some sort of revelation. She shifted to perch on the edge of her chair and then waved her finger side to side at him. "Oh no... Oh no you don't..." She gingerly rose to her feet and began to pace. "Not after all these years." She shook her head and then pierced him with a look that he recognized as the one Minerva would adopt when she was about to spear his heart with a truth. "You're too late."

It was Kent who asked the question that was on the tip of Anthony's tongue. "Has Minerva shared with you her plans?"

"She may have." Aunt Adelaide turned to face her nephew. "But you'll not find out what they are from me."

Kent got to his feet. "Aunt Adelaide." He trailed the woman as she continued to pace about in a circle. "I'm pleading with you. We need to know if Minerva plans to venture to the Americas with you."

Aunt Adelaide continued to shake her head.

Kent tried again. "I won't deny her the adventure to explore the world, but I do need your assurance that you both plan on returning."

"Why is our return of any importance?" Aunt Adelaide rounded on Kent. "You are married. Diana is too. Isadora shall be before long. Gregory and Paul are in no need of mothering."

"Because we love you. We need you both in our lives."

Kent's pleas appeared to fall short. Aunt Adelaide bowed her head. "You have Phyllis. You don't need Minerva or me."

Kent reached for his aunt's elbow and halted her pacing. "That's frankly not true. And the idea of Minerva falling in love with some lout over there and never returning gives me hives."

The sweet and biddable woman that always had an encouraging word whirled around and gave Kent the most wonderful, heartfelt hug.

She released him and marched to stand before Anthony. "Why should I share with you her plans?"

"Because I love her." Anthony raked a hand through his hair and held his breath as he waited for her reaction.

"Bah. You've loved her for years. You are no dullard, no matter what others might say. You are self-aware and are attuned to those around you, so I'll ask one last time: why should I betray my niece's confidence?"

The woman's compliments were as shocking as her direct question. All these years, he had underestimated Aunt Adelaide. Appalled at his lack of insight, Anthony sighed. "I have no good reason, except that the threat of never seeing Minerva again has my heart palpitating. I've finally come to my senses. Minerva is critical to my very existence. I know it is selfish of me to—"

Aunt Adelaide raised a hand in the air and halted his monologue. She moved to the corner of the room and tugged on the bell pull. "I'll ring for tea. If you would care to join me, I'll share with you both what little I know." As if she'd aged ten years, Aunt Adelaide resumed her seat and sighed.

Mere moments later, a maid appeared in the doorway with a tray laden with a tea set. The young maid placed the items on the table next to Aunt Adelaide and scurried from the room.

Aunt Adelaide poured the brown liquid with artful grace.

"Minerva is a clever girl. She hasn't shared a single detail with me as to what exactly she has planned. But she did mention on one of her visits that her future is everything that her current life is not."

Kent took the tea his aunt offered. "Diana is the master of riddles, not I. Pray, explain."

"Anthony will have to do the honors of deciphering Minerva's riddle, for I too am at a loss as to what your sister intends." She handed Anthony a cup and saucer.

"My thanks, Aunt Adelaide." He stared down into the brown liquid. A few stray tea leaves sank to the bottom of his cup. "What does a lady lack in life?"

"Freedom," Aunt Adelaide answered.

In unison, Anthony and Kent repeated, "Freedom?"

"Did I stutter?" Aunt Adelaide shook her head.

"No, Aunt Adelaide, you did not." Anthony stood and moved to resume his position by the window.

Kent leaned back and rested his elbow on the arm of the settee. "My sister enjoys many freedoms already. I don't understand what more she could possibly wish for."

"That is because you are a gentleman, an heir to a viscount." Aunt Adelaide sipped on her tea and speared Anthony with a look over her still-steaming drink. "And you...an earl, should have already married and sired an heir."

If he could have assured Minerva's health and safety, he would have married her years ago. He needed to return to his lodgings and mull over what Minerva could have possibly meant by a future that was everything that her current life was not.

"I think it is time I took my leave." He bowed in Aunt Adelaide's direction. "My thanks for the tea and the edification."

Kent remained seated. "I shall catch up with you later, my friend. I want to spend a little more time with my aunt."

Anthony marched out to the street. It wasn't a question of whether or not he'd be able to decipher Minerva's riddle but whether he could before the completion of their chess game.

CHAPTER TWELVE

THE DRAWING ROOM at the Malbury townhouse was a hive of activity. Surrounded by her family and soon-to-be family members—Gregory, Isadora, Diana, Chestwick, Avondale, and Charlotte—Minerva was struck with a pang of anxiety. If she were to win her matches with Camdon and Anthony, she'd be free to assume the role of Madame Rose, but she would be excluded from these intimate gatherings.

She raised her cup of tea and took a sip of the warm liquid, to chase away the chill that had descended down her back.

Isadora addressed the group. "I suggest we review what we do know of Camdon, rather than continue to speculate on aspects of the man we don't know." Her statement garnered a round of nods.

Chestwick, who was normally one to observe rather than offer an opinion, said, "I know nothing of the man, except that he was rather taken by Minerva at dinner the other eve."

If Charlotte had not been sitting directly in front of her, Minerva might have missed the slight clenching of her sister's hand upon the quill as she meticulously scribbled on the parchment before her. The designated secretary, Charlotte had listened intently to every comment and assumption made by the others all afternoon. And not once had she displayed a reaction until Chestwick's last remark. It was a telltale sign she knew way more about Lord Camdon than what she'd led the others to believe.

"I believe it's time for some much-needed fresh air." Minerva rose from the settee and deposited her cup and saucer on the refreshments cart. "Lady Charlotte, would you care to accompany me for a stroll in the gardens?" Ignoring the stares of concern, Minerva walked directly in front of the settee to stand by Charlotte, who was seated at the desk, and whispered, "I think it best if we discuss Lord Camdon in private."

Charlotte's gaze went to straight to Avondale. Minerva studied the pair. Just as she could read the minds of her siblings, it appeared Charlotte could communicate without words with her brother.

Avondale's near-imperceptible nod had Charlotte smiling up at Minerva. "That's a grand idea." The girl made a show of gathering up the sheets of parchment that contained the notes from the afternoon's discussions. Once she had them all arranged into a neat stack, she looped her arm through Minerva's and the pair set off for the gardens.

It wasn't until they were outdoors and venturing down the garden path that Charlotte began to read from the paper she held steadily in her hands. "Lord Joshua David Chapman, the Earl of Camdon. Age: seven and twenty. Family: father and mother deceased, older brother deceased, elder sister married to Baron William Stenton—they have three boys. Camdon also has three younger brothers: Nathan, who is four and twenty, Samuel, who is three and twenty, and Zachary, who recently turned twenty."

With time running out, Minerva didn't have time to waste or play games with her soon-to-be sister-in-law. She needed to take the situation in hand, so she lifted the stack of papers from Charlotte's hands and glanced over the top sheet. "I must say, you have lovely penmanship—however, mayhap you could share with me details I won't find in my latest copy of *Debrett's*."

Charlotte withdrew her arm and stopped in front of a rose-bush. With a sigh, she clasped her hands behind her back and tipped her chin to her chest in thought. "Your request poses a problem for me."

Minerva smiled and replied, "Because you are an agent for the Foreign Office, and you are loyal to your leader. So if you provide me with the information I need to win, it could be viewed as an act of subterfuge."

"Exactly."

"Very well. Would you be willing to share with me your personal views on Lord Camdon? You need not provide specifics."

Charlotte's brow wrinkled. "I suppose I could share my opinions. Lord Camdon is an extremely skilled agent. His ability to adopt whatever persona is necessary comes as naturally to him as breathing. His distaste for failure, combined with his unfailing patience, will make him a formidable opponent."

"You should have more faith in me."

"Beg pardon?"

"I know how important it is to you for me to win." Minerva smiled and asked, "How long have you been in love with Lord Camdon?"

Charlotte's shoulders stiffened, and then, with a mischievous grin, she asked, "At what age did you realize your heart belonged to Lord Drake?"

Not at all surprised that the young agent would demand a trade of information, Minerva chuckled. After all, secrets were a spy's best currency. "I believe it was the year he turned twenty and I was fourteen."

"Like Lord Drake, who falsely declares you to be like a little sister to him, Lord Camdon has never treated me like more than an acquaintance in society, and no more than a peer while on assignment. He has done so for the past three years."

Her opponent's treatment of Charlotte sounded all too familiar. Anthony had conducted himself in a similar fashion, only it had been for many more than for three years. Minerva tapped her forefinger on her chin. "Perhaps if I can lure Lord Camdon into believing he is a far superior chess player than I…"

Charlotte shook her head. "That plan won't succeed. He's well aware of your renowned chess strategy, both on and off the board."

"Hmm…" Minerva began to pace. "What if I were able to convince him was in control of the board…" She rounded to walk toward Charlotte once more. "Or I could place a key piece in danger, allowing him to believe I had made a misstep in play."

Charlotte's eyes blazed with hope. "If you were able to achieve the latter, I'd wager his overinflated ego may indeed blind him to your strategy."

It wasn't only her future Minerva was playing for—it was Charlotte's too. An idea to ensure Charlotte didn't have to wait an entire decade before gaining her happiness was forming in Minerva's mind. A boon. If she could manage to extract a promise from the astute lady next to her, the girl might fall for her scheme.

"Would you be willing to place a wager?" Minerva asked.

"Ahh…now I fully understand why the Head of the Foreign Office so desperately wishes to recruit you. You know I'd never turn down a bet. I've completely fallen for your trap. What are the terms of this wager?"

"If I'm able to evade marriage to Lord Camdon utilizing the scheme as we discussed, you shall agree to marry the man when he proposes."

"And what makes you believe Camdon would offer for my hand?"

"He may not, but if he does, I would hate for you to decline as an act of loyalty or out of duty to the Wicked Ladies Salon. Promise." Minerva gazed directly into Charlotte's eyes. The woman's mind was a whirl—calculating odds and evaluating consequences.

"Isadora hinted to the fact that if Tom was to marry her, my brother and I would both become pawns in your chess game of life. At the time I didn't give Isadora's statement credit—in hindsight, I should've paid closer attention to her warning."

Charlotte was biding her time. Stalling with gibberish and flattery.

Seeing to a family member's happiness was what brought Minerva joy. If she married Anthony she could continue to do so, but if Anthony lost and she won, it would be six to seven months before she could resume her life as a lady on the shelf.

Minerva waited for Charlotte to respond. Ultimately, she knew Charlotte would agree; it was only a matter of how hard she should push. "Do I have your word?"

"Given the fact Camdon is not easily persuaded to do anything he doesn't want to… Aye, you have my promise to wed the buffoon should he ask me to marry." Charlotte shook her head. "I don't suppose you will share with me why you would seek out such a preposterous promise."

Lord Camdon returning Charlotte's affinity wasn't as unbelievable as Charlotte believed. But it wasn't for Minerva to convince the young lady—that was up to Lord Camdon.

"My reasoning is of no consequence, but know this: I'd never wish a loveless marriage upon any woman, and most definitely not upon you, who is about to join my family." Keeping her answers vague was key to evading the truth. Minerva looped her arm through Charlotte's and headed back inside. "Let's return and join the others, but I promise you this: no sister of mine shall ever marry for anything but love." She would never wish a fate similar to that of her mother's upon anyone. A loveless union led to loneliness, and, in turn, transformed a sweet woman into a bitter one.

As they crossed the threshold into the drawing room, Charlotte asked, "What of you? Will you marry for love?"

If Minerva were to marry, the answer would be a definite yes.

But again avoiding answering the question directly, Minerva replied, "Love is unpredictable, unlike a game of chess. I think I'll stick to playing chess and leave falling in love to others."

Charlotte stared at her for a moment and then said, "I confess that is not the response I was expecting, and it shall take me more than a mere moment for me to scrutinize your meaning. Regardless, I shall eagerly await your match with Camdon this eve."

Minerva remained in the doorway, while Charlotte joined her family, who greeted her return with warm smiles.

A year ago, Minerva had firmly believed in her plan to seek out the life of Madame Rose for a Season. She was no fool. There was no way she could leave her family and her life forever, but one Season of freedom to go about and do as she pleased would provide her with enough joy to last her for the rest of her days. Except Anthony's challenge, his declaration of love, his drugging kisses, had her questioning her resolve.

Heat rose to her cheeks. If she were distracted, Lord Camdon would have an advantage. What she needed to do was focus on the game and the man she was to play this eve, and worry about the rest tomorrow.

If only she could cease the images of Anthony kissing her that crept into her thoughts.

CHAPTER THIRTEEN

ALONE IN HIS chambers, Anthony frowned at his own image in the mirror. Minerva's words replayed over and over in his mind.

Fight for what you want.

He wanted Minerva and he was prepared to do what he must to win her hand.

He'd gained Kent's blessing, eliminating one of his reasons for not having claimed her as his intended in the past. But with one obstacle removed, he was faced with another. Minerva's match with Camdon. Her opponent had the uncanny ability to lure his opponents into complacency and then trounce them at their own game. Camdon would not be as easy for Minerva to defeat as her prior suitors.

Plagued by the issue of her wanting to conduct their game in secret. Anthony glared at his reflection and asked, "Do *you* know why Minerva wants to hide the outcome of our match from others?"

He shook his head and turned his back to the man in the mirror. None of the explanations he had conceived for her peculiar request had proven to be of sound mind, and Minerva always acted with reason and logic.

Anthony turned around once more and peered at the man in front of him, recalling a statement Kent had shared with him once—*a person in love may not always behave as they normally would.* His own actions had proven that.

Reasoning that he'd already broken his promise to remain in the shadows, he formulated a plan to show Minerva what lengths he was prepared to go to in order to fight for what he truly wanted. It was a simple plan. He would accompany Kent and Phyllis to the Harmon Ball, observe Minerva trouncing Camdon, and then publicly issue his own challenge, in effect declaring his intent to marry Minerva before all and sundry. No more loving her in secret. No more observing from afar. It was time he revealed his true self.

His stomach ached as if he had drunk a case of brandy. He fed the last button of his waistcoat through its hole. Fear of failure and rejection began to plague him.

The scratch at his chamber door followed by Kent's bellow from below spurred Anthony to cease daydreaming and jam his arms through his coat. The door of his chamber flung open just as he reached for the latch.

A slightly disheveled Kent frowned at him. "Ready to come out of hiding?"

Anthony nodded. "Do you think I still have a chance?"

Kent slung his arm around Anthony's shoulders. "Camdon is a fine strategist, but I believe my sister shall prevail."

Walking out to the waiting carriage, Anthony tugged on his collar and shook off the sense of foreboding. He entered the coach and nodded at Kent's lovely wife. "A good eve to you, Phyllis. How are you feeling?"

"Concerned." One-word replies were a good indication that the speaker was annoyed or upset.

He studied Phyllis closely as he settled into the rear-facing seat. Even in the dimly lit coach, he could see the worry lines about her eyes. He asked, "Who are you concerned about?"

"Minerva, of course." Phyllis glared at him. "If Camdon succeeds, she'll be forced to marry a stranger! She deserves more, much more."

His smile was replaced with a scowl. Did she not think he was good enough for Minerva?

With wide-eyed shock, Phyllis reached for Kent's arm. "Are you sure this man is not an imposter? Drake would never dare to try to intimidate me with a look. No, this man can't be Drake. The Drake I know employs charm rather than intimidation in order to gain favor."

Kent patted his wife's hand. "I can assure you, the man before you is indeed Anthony MacMillian, the Earl of Drake. He is simply on edge this eve."

"Hm. Well, I prefer the always amicable Drake to the beast seated opposite me. I wonder which Minerva will fancy more."

Phyllis' last remark seized Anthony's heart. What would Minerva think of his appearance tonight?

⋙⋘

THE HARMON BALLROOM was for all intents and purposes empty. The dance floor was devoid of couples. Matchmaking matrons were mysteriously missing. Where was everyone this eve?

What Anthony really wanted to know was: where the devil were Minerva and Camdon?

Behind Kent and Phyllis, Anthony spied Lord Harmon approaching. "Lord Kent. Lady Kent. How lovely to see you this eve." The host frowned as he noticed Anthony. "Lord Drake. I wasn't aware you were in Town."

"I've been keeping my own company of late." Anthony stepped to the side and pointedly scanned the ballroom. Aside from the smattering of wallflowers gathered in small clusters and engaged in rather animated conversations, there wasn't a single soul interested in the fine notes coming from the orchestra. In fact, there wasn't gentleman in sight. Who was at the center of tonight's gossip?

Lord Harmon moved to stand next to Anthony and asked,

"Searching for someone?" The middle-aged gentleman was no fool; he was simply being difficult.

Anthony arched a brow in Lord Harmon's direction and then turned on his heel to leave the group to search for Minerva.

From behind, Lord Harmon said, "Ah…Lord Drake…I'd turn about and head to your left. That is, if you are interested in a certain chess match that has everyone gathered in the card room."

Hands fisted at his sides, Anthony turned and marched back toward the group. As he passed Lord Harmon, the host muttered, "You won't be able to see anything. The room is overcrowded."

Anthony dismissed Lord Harmon's observation. He was skilled at maneuvering through a crowded room unnoticed, and this would be no different.

Except he found himself sighing deeply as he approached the line of guests spilling out from the card room. Lord Harmon hadn't exaggerated. Damn.

He began his quest and squeezed through the crowd. The enormous sums gentlemen were wagering on the outcome would put some of them in dun territory, and combined with the titters of enthusiastic support for Minerva from the ladies behind their fans, this explained why every guest had abandoned their usual posts and were gathered about. His progress slowed the closer he got to the center of the room, where he gathered the match was to take place.

There wasn't a card table in sight. The room was filled with black evening coats standing shoulder to shoulder, with the ladies waving their fans to ward off the muggy heat of the congested room.

Still not close enough to see either Minerva or Camdon, he continued to skillfully maneuver his way through the crowd. He attempted to not draw attention to himself. However, not surprisingly, his serious features were met with curious stares and looks of disbelief as he jostled gentlemen and trod on ladies' toes.

Undeterred, he continued to barge his way toward the chess

table. He had to reach Minerva before the match commenced. The tips of his ears prickled. Kent and Phyllis weren't far behind him. He caught the pair issuing a series of "Beg pardon" and "Please excuse Lord Drake" as they walked behind him.

A sour feeling settled in his stomach. Mansville. The wretched man was nearby. Anthony stopped and scanned the room for Minerva's tormentor. He spied the callous gentleman seated slumped, arms crossed and sulking in the chair next to Avondale. Mansville reminded Anthony of the naughty boys placed on display next to the headmaster during his days at Harrow.

The Duke of Avondale wasn't his favorite neighbor, but given the man's engagement to Isadora, Anthony had resolved himself to be amicable toward the man who had been nothing but a thorn in his side for years, plaguing him with offers from the Head of the Foreign Office.

He resumed wedging his way through the standing bodies until he reached the rows of seats positioned in two semicircles on either side of the chessboard. Minerva and Camdon were already seated and conversing. Why were they chatting rather than playing?

Anthony edged his way closer. The air around the chessboard and the spectators close by hummed with a tension and energy that was present at each and every one of Minerva's public matches. Ladies and gentlemen that considered themselves chess enthusiasts were at the ready to criticize the play of Minerva, who had for years reigned as chess master despite the theorem that a man's mind was far superior to that of a lady's.

A few more steps and he'd be up front and in plain sight. He held his breath, uncertain of what Minerva's reaction to his public appearance would be. The tension in his chest from being separated from her eased as he approached. What a dullard he'd been all these years for not publicly declaring his affection for her before.

Kent and Phyllis had caught up and were right behind him.

Slightly out of breath, Phyllis scolded him, "You could have at least attempted to say 'excuse me.' You ruined at least a half-dozen pairs of slippers along our trek."

He was in no mood for lectures on etiquette. "I'd rather seek out forgiveness than ask for permission to trod upon toes this eve." Anthony continued to forge a path to the front.

"Gah. You are a bear tonight." Phyllis peered around him and then tugged on his sleeve.

He stopped and turned to face her. "What?"

She turned him by the shoulders, and Camdon glanced up in his direction and nodded. His friend's assessing gaze held a devilish twinkle—the man was always on the hunt for a challenge. Anthony took a moment and noted Camdon was seated in front of the black-lacquered pieces, which meant Minerva had the advantage of starting first.

Anthony returned his friend's greeting with a curt nod of his own and then turned his attention to Minerva. She was dressed in a pale green gown he'd never seen before. Unlike most, Minerva wasn't opposed to wearing a gown more than once, preferring to allocate the Malbury modiste funds to her younger sisters. He'd suspected it was all part of Minerva's plan to get Isadora and Diana wed first, but he questioned his presumption when she continued the practice even after Diana happily tied the knot with Chestwick. Minerva's selflessness knew no bounds.

His gaze narrowed on the woman his heart ached for. What aspect of her life was she seeking to escape from?

He blinked. Candlelight from the chandelier above glittered off the diamonds strung through Minerva's coiffure. She was absolutely stunning this evening. Confidence radiated from the woman. Minerva was unnervingly calm and composed. He willed her to look up, but she was methodically adjusting her pieces into perfectly straight lines. Why was she ignoring him?

Minerva sat back and turned slightly to her right, and finally met Anthony's gaze. She arched a brow and then flicked her gaze to three empty seats next to Chestwick and Diana in the front row.

How in the blazes had Minerva known to expect his arrival?

Anthony glanced over his shoulder. Kent shrugged, but Phyllis' beaming smile told him she was responsible for alerting Minerva in advance of his plans. He led the happily married couple over to the empty chairs and slid into the one next to Chestwick.

Chestwick leaned to his left and whispered, "You're late."

"And yet I've managed to be on time for the first move."

"You should know Camdon sequestered me away for hours late this afternoon. It was worse than being interrogated by the French." Chestwick's body shook at his mention of Britain's enemy.

Diana peered around her husband and whispered, "This won't be like any of Minerva's previous matches. Camdon won't be easily defeated."

"It comes as no surprise to me that Camdon wished to gain information regarding your match with Minerva," Anthony said. "He is well trained, and I'd expect nothing less." He shifted in his seat to observe Chestwick and Diana's reaction to his next statement. "Camdon shall make a fine brother-in-law, wouldn't you agree?"

Diana sat back and scowled at Camdon, while Chestwick grinned and replied, "Camdon may be a worthy opponent, one that might even have a chance of winning, but I have faith my sister-in-law shall prevail and gain what she seeks."

Anthony's plan had backfired. He found it was he who was stunned. "Minerva's shared her plans with you?"

Chestwick ignored his question and sat back as his wife leaned over to speak to Anthony once more. "You had best do the right thing if Minerva wins this eve." Diana huffed and sat back, crossing her arms over her chest.

He fully intended to. He would challenge her in front of their peers...and he would win. But he couldn't marry her until he discovered, and ensured she gained, whatever escapade she desperately sought. He had to. If he couldn't give her the family she deserved, he'd give her the adventure she wanted.

He studied Chestwick for another moment. The man's features revealed nothing. What did he know of Minerva's plans?

Minerva's sweet voice caught Anthony's attention. "Lord Camdon, shall we begin?"

Camdon scanned the crowd around them and then nodded. "Ready."

Gloveless, Minerva hovered a steady hand over the center pawn and shifted it two spaces forward.

Chestwick commented, "Relax. I expect this to be a rather lengthy match."

Anthony prayed Chestwick was wrong. He was counting on Minerva to make swift, decisive moves and cursorily dispatch her opponent.

Except Minerva's cheeks were glowing pink, and there was a distinct lack of tension in her neck. Where was the woman who detested being the center of attention, who let the presence of Mansville and his lot make her hand shake, who was on edge when playing a stranger? Peculiar.

Minerva made her move, relaxed back into her seat, and smiled at her opponent. Not smiled, beamed at Camdon as if they were close friends, not mere acquaintances.

Had she decided to let the man win, and wed Camdon? Bile rose to his throat at the thought.

Chestwick mumbled, "What the blazes is Camdon up to? Moving his pawn, but only one space."

Anthony refocused his attention on the chessboard rather than Minerva. His heart thumped in his chest as she moved her king pawn two spaces forward to join the first. Her first two moves were textbook in nature, no surprises. Camdon's gaze was trained on Minerva and not the board. It was clear his play was dictated by his assessment of his opponent, not the position of the pieces. The seasoned spy leaned forward before briefly glancing down at the board then studying Minerva once more.

Anthony forced his muscles to relax, as Chestwick had advised. This would be the longest and hardest game of chess he'd have to endure in silence.

Finally, Camdon inhaled and then reached for his bishop and placed it in the space his pawn had vacated. A bold and aggressive second move. The man's gaze flickered to Minerva the entire time he was making his move. Observing her. Assessing her. Appreciating her.

Anthony crossed his arms and jammed his fists tight into his armpits. Damn Camdon. His untraditional moves may prove to be effective if Minerva wasn't careful.

"Hmm." Chestwick leaned over and asked, "What would your next move be if you were Minerva?"

Anthony studied the board. "I'd mimic Camdon and move my bishop." Before he even completed the statement, Minerva executed the move he would have made.

"It appears Minerva and you do think alike," Chestwick commented.

It wasn't uncommon for chess players to foretell his or her opponent's next move—that was what distinguished serious chess strategists from those that played for purely recreational purposes. What was disturbing was that Camdon's play was somewhat reckless, in Anthony's opinion, and that was incongruent with what he knew of the man he considered a friend. Even Avondale and Mansville looked on with their brows furrowed.

Everyone around the room appeared somewhat perplexed—everyone, that was, but Minerva and Lady Charlotte. The pair gave Anthony the impression that Camdon was playing exactly as they'd expected.

The corner of Minerva's lips twitched as Camdon moved one of his pawns two spaces forward, placing it in jeopardy. As soon as Minerva took Camdon's pawn, the man sat back, crossed his leg over his knee, and reviewed the remaining pieces.

Anthony glanced at Chestwick. "What do you predict Camdon will do?"

Chestwick shrugged. "Not a clue, but the gleam in Minerva's eyes tells me he is playing exactly as she had hoped."

Anthony thought the same. While everyone waited for Camdon to act, Anthony sat back and admired Minerva. There was an air of confidence surrounding her this eve. She easily ignored Mansville's interest, and she was more focused on the crowd than the wood pieces in front of her. Chess was Minerva's favorite pastime; she would obsess over analyzing and replaying matches long after they had been played. What was her preoccupation with the guests gathered about this eve?

Camdon unfolded his leg and firmly placed it back on the floor, before reaching for his bishop once more to capture Minerva's pawn that sat on the front line.

Without hesitation, Minerva picked up her queen and made her move. "Check." She glanced up at Anthony and gave him a wink.

Anthony blinked, registering that if it had been him she had been playing, he would now owe her a secret. And truth be told, he would have made the same move as Camdon had. He frowned at the board. Minerva may have placed Camdon in check, but her queen sat vulnerable.

Camdon made the logical move of shifting his pawn one space forward to protect his king and stall defeat. Again, Minerva acted quickly, taking Camdon's pawn with one of her own.

Anthony inwardly groaned at Camdon's smile. The man was clearly planning to take advantage of Minerva's misstep in moving her queen. Except Minerva didn't make mistakes.

Anthony glanced at the chessboard once more. Was Minerva sending him or Camdon a subliminal message? Was she as vulnerable and exposed as her queen?

Camdon lounged back in his chair. When Minerva finally met his gaze, her wily opponent said, "I gather you are eager to finish the game quickly this eve, given your quick and decisive moves."

"While I love the game of chess, I also enjoy a dance or two"—she made a point of looking around at the guests—"and it appears there are others who share the sentiment."

Camdon leaned closer over the board, pretending to study the pieces. Thankfully, Anthony was able to read lips, for the man spoke so quietly that no one but Minerva would hear him say, "They are free to do as they please. No one is forcing them to stay."

Mirroring her challenger's actions, Minerva replied, "Afraid you shall lose?"

Anthony didn't care for the intimate nature of their verbal sparring. Minerva's eyes were alight with interest. Damn Camdon and his mysterious allure.

Camdon replied, "Not in the least. In fact, I believe I'm in a prime position to win." He reached for his knight and placed it next to Minerva's pawn, at the ready to take her piece.

The significance of the pieces that both Minerva and Camdon had chosen to play wasn't lost on Anthony—pawns, bishops, the knight, and the queen. He simply hadn't figured out if he was the bishop or the knight.

Minerva tilted her head slightly and pierced Anthony with a stare and a breathtaking smile. He gathered that her actions meant she was going to place Camdon in check once more, but how?

She answered his silent question, moving her pawn forward to take the pawn protecting Camdon's king but leaving her queen primed and ready for the taking. Minerva whispered, "Check."

A trickle of dread ran down Anthony's spine. Again, if he were her opponent, he'd be indebted to yet another secret. He would have owed her two, while he would have gained none of hers, for Anthony was in total agreement with Camdon's play thus far—and the man was about to lose.

It was clear Camdon was oblivious to Minerva's scheme. The man grinned and moved his knight to take her queen.

Minerva had lured Camdon's attention away and sacrificed her queen to win.

She shifted slightly and straightened her back, as if she was partially shocked at having lost her queen. Anthony shook his head. She was a far better actress than he had thought.

Utilizing her signature move, Minerva tapped her forefinger to her chin, feigning contemplation until they all heard Mansville's gasp. That was her cue—Minerva reached for her bishop hiding behind her pawn and placed it in the diagonal between Camdon's knight and king. "Checkmate."

Camdon rose to his feet and offered his hand to assist Minerva to stand. "Well played, my lady. Perhaps you will grant me a dance to soothe my aching heart."

"It would be my pleasure, my lord."

Chestwick's hand landed solidly at the center of Anthony's back, sending him lurching forward. "If I was to guess, Minerva intends to take you down next. That is, if I interpreted the game correctly and you were indeed Camdon's knight."

Diana stood and nodded. "Husband, there is no question in my mind as to what my sister plans next. Defeat Drake and win her freedom to do as she pleases."

Chestwick rose and wrapped and arm about his wife. "And has marriage prevented you from doing what you please?"

Diana swatted her husband's chest and giggled. "You know very well it hasn't."

Anthony's mind was spinning. The loving couple's exchange had reminded him of the type of marriage he longed for and confirmed his suspicions that Minerva had no intention of intentionally losing their match. Not only must he win her hand in the chess game, he'd have to win her heart back too.

Mansville slid into the seat next to Anthony. The room was empty. How long had he remained staring at the chessboard?

"Are you going to challenge Lady Minerva?"

"What interest do you have in the matter?" Anthony turned to face the vile man that had tormented Minerva for the past three years.

"Lady Minerva threatens us all. Men are the superior sex, and she needs to be reminded of the fact."

Mansville was an idiot. Anthony stood. "I'd advise you to continue to keep your distance from Lady Minerva, and once she's my wife, you had best never go near her again."

"Careful, Drake—your best friend Kent and his lot will need votes this session."

"My days of being agreeable and neutral are over. If you fail to heed my warning, I can assure you, your vote will no longer hold any weight. It is you who shall need to be careful going forward." Anthony swiveled and left the room, determined to find Minerva. He was intent on the task at hand—publicly challenging Minerva to a chess match. A match that should have taken place years ago.

CHAPTER FOURTEEN

*B*REATHE.

Minerva focused on her dance partner's cravat. She could ignore the curious looks from others with ease when seated with a chessboard in front of her and a game to focus on. But dancing in the arms of the charming Lord Camdon, Minerva couldn't block out the whispers that were no doubt about her. Her ears burned. She sensed their gazes, heating the skin on the back of her neck. They were waiting…waiting for her to make a mistake.

Oh, she could sing and dance in front of them when she donned a fake beauty spot and wore face paint without issue. But in a ballroom full of her peers, when a simple gaze held a moment too long or a smile a little too broad could, in a blink of an eye, transform into the latest *on-dit* or, even worse, result in a couple finding themselves in front of a reverend, every inch of exposed skin on the back of her neck burned from their gazes.

Her sisters Isadora and Diana whirled around her, led by their beaus effortlessly. Minerva reminded herself—*I won. No matter what occurs, no one can make me marry.* She willed her feet to move.

At the light pressure applied to her hand that was securely captured in Lord Camdon's grasp, Minerva glanced up at her dance partner. "Would it be too much to request another boon from you personally, Lord Camdon?"

"Is securing the word of the Head of the Foreign Office not to meddle in your affairs and wounding my pride not enough?" Lord Camdon's smile was dazzling and put her at ease. He was a gracious loser, not at all like her previous challengers, who took exception to being defeated by a woman.

"I believe you're not half as wounded as you claim to be," Minerva replied, and then added with all seriousness, "I'm quite certain you've endured and survived much worse." Conversing with Lord Camdon eased the tension in her muscles. She weaved through the line of gentleman dancers and met the gazes of the other guests with a new perspective.

"Ah, but the injury I've incurred this eve has not merely been to my pride. And it's been a long while since I've been denied something I truly desire."

She returned to stand before Lord Camdon. He wanted her? Standing face to face with him, she studied her dance partner's features. His serious eyes held a twinkle of impatience.

No. The man didn't want her. If she were to hazard a guess as to Lord Camdon's true motivations, she would place a sizable wager that he simply didn't wish to expend the time or energy on finding a suitable wife.

She caught sight of Charlotte standing on the fringes of the dance floor holding court among a gaggle of young bucks. Hm. Charlotte could bring Lord Camdon up to snuff, but *would* she, was the real question.

Minerva stepped forward and began to circle Lord Camdon. "If marriage is what you desire, then I suggest you merely look around—there are multiple eligible ladies surrounding us at this moment."

When she came around, his intense gaze bored into her. "Ah, but is there another who is daring enough to risk spinsterhood, all in the hopes to gain a worthy husband?"

"Skilled chess players are often accused of hyper focus, unable to see alternatives once a stratagem has been formed in their mind. I was guilty of such. That was until I was forced to see the alternatives that were, in fact, right before me."

Camdon's brows knitted. He took her word seriously. A rarity. After a moment, he said, "You believe I have misjudged someone. Mayhap even someone I'm already acquainted with. Who is this mysterious lady?"

"What would be the fun in simply telling you? After all, you are a brilliant agent for the Crown, are you not? I have faith you shall figure it out." She took his extended hand and promenaded next to him. Bolstered by the confidence that she was able to ignore the prying gazes of onlookers, she said, "As to the boon I would like to request…"

"Speaking of being singularly minded." He tugged her a little closer and smiled down at her.

A flutter in her chest caused her to gasp—Drake was close by. She scanned the ballroom as Camdon spun her in a circle until she was once again face to face with her grinning dance partner. The tension in her neck diminished. Lord Camdon was rather skilled at placing others at ease. "I already admitted to possessing the trait in spades. However, at present, I need your assistance in avoiding Drake this eve."

She expected Lord Camdon to search the room for Drake, but instead his full attention remained on her. "Fear he may challenge you?"

"Oh, I have no doubt he intends to issue a public challenge, and I intend to accept, except I need more time to…well, to get my affairs in order. Will you help me?"

He studied her for no more than a heartbeat, and then his eyes widened with recognition. "Despite your feelings for Drake, you plan on devising a strategy to defeat him. Why?"

"When I play, I play to win." Her rote response slipped from her lips. It wasn't pride that drove her persistence to win. Or perhaps it was. But if she was to wed, she wanted a man who could not only defeat her but also love her unequivocally.

Lord Camdon leaned in closer. "I understand the sentiment well, but at what cost?"

She gave him a watery smile and said, "Regardless of if I win or lose my match with Drake, I shall pay handsomely in one way or another."

"A conundrum for certain."

Lord Camdon expertly maneuvered them to the opposite side of the dance floor. And Minerva saw her dance partner for what he was: a kindred spirit. He understood without the need for her to explain the complex interconnections that her mind weaved around every situation.

Lord Camdon lightened his hold on her as the last note of the waltz floated in the air. "In return for my assistance tonight, you shall grant me the permission to escort you on a ride in the park tomorrow."

Without hesitation, she said, "Agreed." She spied Anthony in the wings.

"Damn. I should have demanded more."

"Most definitely." She gave him a smile that she only reserved for family. They both halted at the fringes of the crowd. She couldn't see beyond the crush of bodies in front of her, but she could feel Anthony descending upon her quickly.

Able to see over the heads of most, Lord Camdon scanned the crowd. "I'll delay Drake while you take your leave."

With a nod, Minerva left Lord Camdon's side.

Sidestepping, tiptoeing, and even ducking in some instances, she managed to slip through the crowd at an efficient pace. She had no intentions of departing the ball—not yet. She wasn't one to run from a challenge.

She glanced over her shoulder and blinked as Camdon herded guests to block Anthony's progress. It was a sight to witness. It was as if he moved them like pawns. She blinked again. Anthony countered by slipping straight through the middle of the gentlemen, nodding and smiling as he barged his way through. She needed to move faster if her plan was to work, knowing that once Anthony settled upon a plan, he, too, was hard to redirect.

Minerva picked up her skirts and weaved her way around the ballroom, going over her plan to sequester Anthony alone. When

Phyllis had alerted her to Anthony's plan to reemerge, she knew instantly that Drake intended to challenge her publicly. Which meant he had a plan to defeat her.

She muttered a sincere "Pardon me" to every guest that glowered at her as she passed by. It had been necessary to set aside her fears during her match with Lord Camdon, but now that was done, Minerva couldn't shake the image of Anthony placing her in check and winning. Fear trickled down her spine. She wasn't sure if the fear she was experiencing stemmed from the possibility that her dream of becoming Madame Rose for the Season would never come to fruition, or if it was from the prospect of wedding Anthony and his discovering the truth about Madame Rose.

She needed privacy. A quiet place to think, analyze, and weigh the various outcomes.

CHAPTER FIFTEEN

Hide-and-seek had been one of Minerva's favorite holiday games to play out at Malbury Manor. And it appeared the woman had yet to outgrow her fondness for the entertainment, for she was leading Anthony on a merry chase around the ballroom.

Another wave of guests rolled his way. Rather than plunging into the sea of bodies, he stood still as gentlemen escorted their partners around him. Delayed for a moment, he rolled onto his toes and searched the room. Where in the blazes was Minerva headed?

As the bodies around him ebbed, he pushed forward and came face to face with Camdon.

"Drake, my old friend."

He didn't have time for idle chatter. Anthony stepped into the center of the small, intimate group of gentlemen gathered. Each of them were seasoned spies. Some he believed were linked to the Home Office, while the others were associated with the Foreign Office, like Camdon.

In a low whisper for their ears only, Anthony said, "I'd advise your respective leaders to honor Minerva's request."

He waited for each man to nod before continuing to pursue his future wife. He made his way to the edge of the dance floor. Minerva was weaving her way toward the terrace doors. Why would she attempt to slip away to the gardens? She wouldn't. The risk of prying eyes catching them together alone in the garden was far too great.

However, if she wanted to send him on a wild goose chase, she'd lead him to believe she was venturing into the dark. He stopped. Where would he go if he needed a moment alone?

He turned on his heel and ceased following her.

As he passed the refreshments table, Kent stepped forward in front of him, stalling his progress. "Where are you going?"

Anthony frowned at his best friend and said, "I'm off to find Minerva."

"You're headed in the wrong direction." Kent nodded in the direction of the gardens.

"I don't believe she intends to take a stroll in the gardens. I'm convinced she's plotting, and she merely wants us to believe that is her intended destination."

He attempted to step around Kent, but the man took a step simultaneously and blocked Anthony from leaving. "Just in case I'm right and you're wrong for once, I'll go check."

Kent stepped to stand beside his wife and whispered into her ear. Phyllis glared at Anthony before looping her arm through her husband's, and the pair marched as one toward the terrace doors, a couple with a common purpose and in total accord. A rarity amongst the *ton*. Except the Malbury siblings, who had each sworn to never marry unless it was for love…and not surprisingly, to date, they each had upheld their word. Minerva would never break an oath, and Anthony was going to ensure she never had to.

He swiveled, clasped his hands behind his back, and skirted around guests until he was marching down the hall, back to the drawing room where Minerva and Camdon had played their match. Following his instincts, he stood in the now-empty firelit room and stared at the chessboard.

If he had assessed the situation correctly, Minerva would be along shortly. In the meantime, he wanted to replay her match with Camdon once more. He sat in the seat Camdon had occupied earlier and studied the pieces, reassessing each of Camdon's moves. The moves that he himself would have played. He couldn't afford to make the same mistakes in his own game with Minerva, for if he lost their game, he would be sacrificing the most important person in his life.

Sacrifice.

His mind and heart raced as he pinpointed the move that had ensured Minerva victory—the surrender of her queen. It was a message. Referred to as the Ice Queen, Minerva may appear to be yielding, when in fact she was planning to do the complete opposite.

Damn the clever woman.

The soft patter of slippers against the hardwood heralded Minerva's arrival. Anthony stood and faced the woman he desperately wanted.

"How did you know this was my intended destination and not in the gardens?" Minerva slid into the seat opposite him.

He took his seat and replied, "After valiantly winning your freedom, why would you venture into the dark and risk scandal? The gardens made no sense."

She placed her pieces in their original positions. "And what if I had simply wished for fresh air?"

"Then you would have had Camdon escort you instead of sending him off on a foolish errand to try to delay me."

Bishop in hand, Minerva stilled and looked up at him. "There are distinct disadvantages to your knowing me so well."

Anthony picked up her queen that Camdon had captured earlier and twirled it between his fingertips. "Ah…but I would say there are many more advantages than disadvantages."

"Such as?" Minerva sat back in her seat and crossed her arms over her chest.

"Hmm… There are vast number of advantages. Which shall I share first?" He leaned forward and placed her queen in its rightful spot next to her king. "For starters, we are both fully aware of each other's quirks."

Minerva arched a brow at him. "Pray, share what peculiar traits I possess."

Anthony grinned. "I love that you sing and dance with imaginary gentlemen in the gardens when you think no one is around. I love that you blink when doing arithmetic in your head. I love that you hum bawdy ballads while doing needlepoint. I love that you separate your peas on your plate and eat them last. I love—"

"Enough. You've proven your point." Color flooded Minerva's cheeks, and she rose to pace in front of the fire. The flames flickered over her form, highlighting every generous curve.

Unable to stay away, Anthony joined her by the fire. He stopped in front of her and leaned an arm over the mantel. He didn't have time to waste. He needed information, and Minerva was the only one who could provide him with the answers. "Will you share with me what it is exactly that you stand to lose if I were to win our match?" He reached for her hands.

Minerva shrugged and replied, "Besides my pride?"

He gave her hands a squeeze and willed her to trust him and tell him her secrets.

She released a deep sigh and then added, "If I tell you, promise not to laugh."

"Of course I won't. Whatever it is, it is obviously extremely important to you." He took a step forward and gazed down at her. In the firelight he could see the concern in her gaze. "I promise not to laugh."

Her lips parted. He was about to finally discover her plans. His pulse raced and his heart thudded against his ribs. But then she closed her mouth and shook her head.

"I need to know, Minerva. I want to know what it is I'll be denying you should I win." He squeezed her hands once more. "Please. Remember when there were no secrets between the two of us. I've confessed my love for you. I hold no other secrets from you."

Guilt flashed in Minerva's eyes. What secrets had she managed to keep from him?

She released a deep, soul-wrenching sigh. "If you win, I shall have to abandon my plans to live in disguise for the remainder of the Season."

Only Minerva would dare attempt such an elaborate scheme. He asked, "Whom would you be disguised as?"

She tugged her hands free and placed them upon her hips. A spark of defiance or anger—he wasn't sure which—appeared and then quickly disappeared. In a clipped voice, she answered, "Madame Rose."

"Madame Rose! You want to pretend to be the famous opera singer?"

"Who said I'd be an imposter?"

Impossible. Minerva couldn't be Madame Rose. He shook the absurd idea from his head, but when his gaze returned to Minerva—the truth hit him. Minerva and Madame Rose were one and the same. "Bloody hell, Minerva, whom did you set your sights on to be your protector?"

She rolled her eyes. "I'm not in need of a protector."

"If you have no intention of luring a gentleman to sponsor your Season, how do you plan to pay for lodging, food, clothes?"

"I'm an excellent saver. I've amassed enough funds. I merely want one Season to do as I please, and then I'll resolve myself to the role of spinster." She turned away from him and walked back to the chessboard. Minerva picked up a pawn before continuing, "And in time, I'll become my nephews and nieces' favored aunt."

Stunned beyond words, Anthony stared at Minerva as if she were a total stranger. The woman was seriously considering giving up her life as a lady to become a bleeding performer.

Voices out in the hall spurred Anthony out of his stupor. They couldn't be found alone. He marched up to her. She tilted her chin up to meet his gaze.

He leaned down and said, "We are not done with this discussion." As if he needed confirmation she was indeed Madame Rose, he bent and crushed his lips to hers. When she kissed him back and then grazed her tongue over his lower lip, just as the opera singer had done two years ago, Anthony released a groan that was part desire, part submission.

The kiss left no doubt. Minerva was Madame Rose.

He released her and said, "Stay here. I shall return momentarily."

The window was his only escape. He pried the window open, and, without a second thought, he slipped out into the dark.

Thankfully his toes balanced on a ledge, and he shimmied his way along the exterior wall. Memories of the night he'd spent lying abed with Madame Rose two years ago, fully dressed, fully aroused, flashed before him, slowing his progress. How could he have not known it was Minerva? Argh. What a fool he was. He had lain next to her—no, not Minerva, next to Madame Rose—and confessed that while he was extremely attracted to her, he could not be intimate because he was in love with his best friend's sister. As Madame Rose, the chit had dragged a solitary finger along his jaw and whispered, "No one will know." But he couldn't betray Minerva and had rolled away, leaving the opera singer's backstage room.

Damnation. He rested his forehead against the cool exterior stone—Minerva had known all these years he was in love with her, and she never confessed. Anthony didn't know if should be angry, relieved, or incensed at the woman.

He glanced down at the empty terrace and jumped to the ground. Before he ran into another guest, he marched straight back to the drawing room, only to find Minerva and the chessboard surrounded by Kent, Chestwick, and a gaggle of young bucks.

He was going to do what he'd originally set out to do this eve. He approached Minerva. The gentlemen parted, making space for him. "Lady Minerva, I'd be honored if you would accept my challenge for your hand."

Minerva avoided his gaze, which was a first. She sank into a curtsy and said, "I accept your challenge, Lord Drake." Straightening, she turned to address Kent. "Brother, I trust you shall make the necessary arrangements."

As soon as Kent nodded, she picked up her skirts and fled, which was utterly surprising, for Minerva preferred to face obstacles, not run from them.

Anthony glanced at Kent, who shrugged and said, "Let's find Phyllis and be off."

As they reentered the ballroom, they found Avondale first. Anthony paused next to the Foreign Office agent and said, "I trust you shall see to it that Minerva arrives home safely."

"Aye. I intend to return both Malbury sisters to their residence as soon as they return from the ladies' retiring room."

Kent returned with Phyllis, who was scowling at Anthony once again. She narrowed her gaze upon him and said, "It's only fair that Minerva be granted a few days to rest before her next match. Your game shall be held at the Malbury residence in three days' time. Observers shall be granted access by invite only."

It was clear Kent wasn't the one in charge. Except Anthony suspected it wasn't Phyllis' idea to delay their match either.

Minerva. The minx was still at the heart of every decision. A three-day delay was fine with him. He'd utilize every moment to his advantage, now that he knew of her plans.

CHAPTER SIXTEEN

HIDDEN UNDER THE bedcovers from the morning light streaming in through her windows, Minerva rolled over and punched her pillow. She placed her cheek in the small indentation she managed to make and sighed.

Sleep had evaded her all night. Her confession replayed over and over in her mind. It had been a mistake to admit to being Madame Rose. She should have reserved her secret in case Anthony placed her in check during their game. What had she been thinking? The dark smudges under his eyes had softened her resolve. That and the burden of guilt she'd carried with her for two long years. She hated deceiving him—knowing the truth and unable to convince him to act upon his feelings for her.

Each and every one of her attempts as Lady Minerva Malbury to spur Anthony into taking action had failed. She decided if she was unable to convince him as herself, she might be able to as Madame Rose. The idea had merit at the time she initially conceived it. But even while she formulated her plan to assume the role of Madame Rose once again, she'd held out hope Anthony would challenge her to a game of chess, and her efforts to lead a double life wouldn't be necessary. Except month after month, she was left disappointed.

That was until Avondale's house party. It was while she was apart from Anthony that she realized, even though he might have been the reason for her scheme, the idea of gaining her independence had become more and more alluring. Her plan had then become more about her than Anthony.

Wide awake, she rolled onto her back and stared up at the canopy above her bed. Anthony. The man who had featured in dreams both day and night. Her eyes fluttered closed, and she reached for a pillow to hug it close to her chest. Vivid images of Anthony passionately kissing her as Madame Rose after one of her performances were no longer fond memories. Now the memory left a bitter taste atop her tongue.

Ugh. She was jealous of her alter ego. It made no sense, especially since he'd declined to pursue her as Madame Rose.

Steady, rhythmic footfalls out in the hall signaled her sister's approach. Minerva tucked the pillow behind her head just as Diana waltzed into her chambers and announced, "Chestwick and Avondale are waiting below."

Minerva rose to a sitting position and stretched her arms above her head. "Waiting for what?"

"To assist you." Diana emerged from the changing chamber with a pretty yellow day dress.

Minerva rubbed the grit from her eyes and swung her feet over the edge until her toes touched the floor. "Sister mine, it is way too early in the morn to speaking in riddles. Pray, explain why you are here or leave."

"Since Drake has recruited Benedict and Camdon to assist him in preparing for your chess match, Isadora and I agreed it's only fair that Chestwick and Avondale come to your aid." Diana placed the dress next the changing screen.

Minerva padded her way to the corner to perform her morning ablutions. Blast. Anthony had recruited her most recent opponent. Lord Camdon would be able to provide a detailed analysis of her play. Her instincts were right: the man was preparing to wage war upon her.

Since Anthony hadn't played in years, it was only fair he be given a chance—not that Camdon or Kent would seriously be able to help. A wiser choice would have been for Anthony to ask Chestwick and Avondale for assistance. Both gentlemen were indeed superb chess players who simply masked their skills rather than flaunt them.

She had asked Phyllis for help in relaying the message that the game was to be delayed. However, she had not specified for how long. Minerva returned to the bed, picked up the bright day dress, and asked, "How many days do I have to prepare?"

"Three."

"Then there is no rush." She sank back onto the bed and flopped backward.

Diana grabbed her hands and pulled her back up to sit. As if she was about to impart a lecture, Diana stared directly at her. "Drake is no fool. He knows you better than anyone, and with instruction from Camdon, he could very well defeat you." Diana's brow knitted into a frown. "Wait. Do you want Drake to win? Have you forgiven him for failing to act these past three years?"

Diana and her sequential questions. Minerva had missed her little sister. She stood and embraced her. "I don't know what I want any longer." She ignored the day dress and donned her robe. "I'm not even certain I have a choice in the matter."

Her sister pulled back to glare at her. "Impossible. You are always telling me that there is an alternative. You have the trust of many; now you must trust yourself to make the right move."

"In this instance I might have positioned myself into a no-win situation." Minerva shook her head and released her sister. She meandered over to the window.

Diana said, "Pray, explain."

Absently Minerva replied, "I can't decide when I've only known but one life."

"I don't understand." Diana joined her by the window.

Minerva had kept this secret of becoming Madame Rose from all for so long, so to share it with Diana would be like giving up a large part of her. But if she wanted to know for certain what life to choose, she'd need the assistance of others.

Her gaze trained on the gardens below, Minerva confessed, "I want to experience life as Madame Rose."

"Egad. You've cost me a sovereign." Diana grinned. "I should have known not to wager against Isadora." She grasped her hands behind her back and strode to the middle of the room, muttering, "I can't believe it. My own sister...the one and only...famous Madame Rose."

Diana whirled about to face Minerva. The admiration in her sister's eyes created within Minerva the same exhilaration as when she sang on stage. It was a relief to finally share her secret.

"Isadora suspected?"

"She did." Diana began to pace and then froze. "Will two nights as Madame Rose suffice?"

"What?" Minerva must have misheard her.

"You helped Isadora and I gain what we wished for, and we shall do the same for you."

As if on cue, Isadora barged into the chambers. "With the assistance of Gregory and the staff, we shall be able to convince Mama. But gaining Gregory's assistance will take more than a bag of coin." A guilty shade of pink was painted across her cheeks. Isadora had been eavesdropping the entire time.

Diana said, "Isadora, mayhap you could host a private event at Wembley Hall."

Her sisters had lost all their wits. Minerva let Isadora and Diana jabber on in the background.

Three days living as Madame Rose.

Three days of freedom to make her own decisions.

Three days apart from her family and the man her heart still ached for.

It would be a test.

Anthony had only managed to stay away from friends and family for less than a week. Would she be capable of staying totally out of sight for three days and two nights?

Minerva quickly assessed the risks and consequences. The

idea warranted an attempt to discover what freedom might be like.

She turned away from the window and said, "I shall convince Gregory to go along with our scheme. And no, I shall not share with either of you how I will go about it." She marched over to her bed and picked up the brightly colored day dress that reflected her mood—sunny and hopeful. "I'll slip away as soon as you and your men depart." She walked over to the door and opened it for her sisters to leave.

Isadora paused in front of the threshold to ask, "But how will we contact you? How will we know you are well?"

"If I don't return in three days, send for the Bow Street Runners. They'll be able to locate me." Minerva shooed them out of her room. "Now off with you both."

Her sisters trudged down the hall a few feet before Diana looked at Isadora and mumbled, "I don't like the twinkle in her eyes."

Isadora linked her arm with Diana's. "I don't either, but we owe Minerva our support."

Minerva shut the door and scurried over to her writing desk. She slid into her chair and pulled out a sheet of crisp white parchment. With no time to waste, she began to pen a note to her brother.

Dear Gregory

You shall claim to all and sundry I'm not to be disturbed or seen for the next few days.

Ensure Kent and Mama believe you, and I shall ensure that your debt to Lord Eversham is settled.

Your loving sister
Minerva

She sealed the note with wax and rushed to hand it off to Jack, who was posted just outside her door. "For Gregory's eyes only, and then I'll need your assistance in a half-hour at the back alley."

Brow furrowed, Jack nodded and then rushed off to deliver the parchment.

Minerva glanced about the room. There was much to do. She was going on an adventure.

CHAPTER SEVENTEEN

WHILE ANTHONY WAS glad to be once again residing in his Mayfair townhome, and drinking in the company of friends, he also wished Kent and Camdon would cease glaring at him. He was well aware of their expectations and wishes—win, win at all costs. Minerva was no ordinary chess player. She was a master strategist both seated in front of a chessboard and in life.

Anthony sat back in his chair and waited for Camdon to make his move while Kent continued to pace in a triangular pattern between the window, the door, and the chessboard. He steepled his fingers and drummed his fingertips. Subtle physical movements were a tactic Minerva often employed to distract her opponents. He needed to compile a list of actions that he could employ during their game.

He leaned forward, crossing and uncrossing his legs. He had yet to distract Camdon, but when his opponent looked up from the board to scowl at Anthony, he knew his latest tactic had worked. Anthony stilled, but as soon as Camdon returned his attention to the board, he resumed the finger tapping. That was until Camdon growled, "Good Lord, man, stop."

Bailey, Anthony's butler, cleared his throat at the doorway and then proceeded to enter the drawing room with precise steps. He presented Kent with a salver that held a note. A missive with the Malbury seal. Was it from Minerva?

Kent picked up the note, turned it over, and lifted it to his nose, which scrunched up as soon as he inhaled. There was no hint of lemon nor vanilla from where Anthony sat, which meant it wasn't from Minerva. Then who was it from?

Exerting his will, Anthony remained seated instead of jumping up and snatching the damn parchment from Kent's fingers.

Kent pried open the letter and said, "Gregory has declared Minerva indisposed for the next few days." He tapped the corner of the parchment against his palm. Brow furrowed, he reread the note.

Camdon peered up from the chessboard. "Is your sister ill?"

"Most likely not. But whatever Minerva is up to, she doesn't want me"—Kent's gaze shifted from Camdon to Anthony—"or us interfering." He tucked the note into his jacket pocket and resumed his pacing. The last time Anthony saw his friend this agitated was when Kent had lost all hope of ever getting Phyllis to give him a second chance. Did Kent not have faith in Anthony to win his match with Minerva? Was he devising another scheme in the event his friend failed?

Anthony rubbed his temples. The issue was that if he were Kent, he'd be doing the exact same. Minerva rarely took to her bed due to an ailment—although the Malbury sisters often used illness as an excuse to avoid accompanying their mama about Town. Half the *ton* believed the ladies were a sickly lot, when in fact the Malbury sisters were healthier than most. They could walk miles without issue, due to years of practice trapsing about the countryside. He would know, since he trailed Minerva about every summer.

Camdon broke into his thoughts, commenting, "Mayhap Minerva simply wishes for you to remain here while she devises stratagems with Chestwick and Avondale to defeat you." Camdon placed Anthony in checkmate with his pawn. "Which is apparently not that difficult."

Kent glanced down at the board and scoffed. "If Drake could concentrate for longer than a minute on the game, he'd have won." He abandoned his pacing and walked over to the sideboard. The clink of crystal as Kent removed the decanter stopper and the splash of liquid into the tumbler had Anthony thinking of his oath to refrain from partaking until after his match with Minerva. No brandy, and definitely none of the aged Scottish whisky he had a preference for. He needed a clear head for his match with Minerva. Except his mind and thoughts were scrambled after his discovering Minerva was Madame Rose.

He had spent most of the night lying in bed reexamining past events. Minerva had tried to tell him many a time, giving hint after hint. Each one obvious to him now that he knew the truth. He had prided himself in being able to decipher puzzles and solve riddles before anyone else, yet he had missed every clue Minerva gave him over the past two years. For two years, he'd been a buffoon. Ashamed of how blind he had been, Anthony craved a drink to drown his embarrassment. How had he failed to see Minerva for the clever minx that she was?

His hand shook as he reset the pieces in front of him. He had acted just as she had accused him of, only seeing what he wanted to believe. Except he knew the truth now, and he still was at a loss as to how to proceed. She wanted to live the life of an actress. How could he grant her wish and marry her at the same time?

Kent raised his glass in the air and gave his thoughts a voice. "It's possible Minerva has agreed to work with Chestwick and Avondale to devise a plan to defeat Drake, but I'd wager Minerva has refused their help and is scheming to go on one last adventure before she is shackled."

"How can you be so certain Drake will win?" Camdon finished realigning his pieces and sat back to accept the glass of amber liquid Kent was offering him.

"Despite his attempts to undermine his abilities, Drake is a blooming genius…" Kent drained his glass and walked back to refill it. "And my sister has been in love with my best friend from the moment I brought him home that first holiday break, years and years ago."

Anthony ignored Kent's comment and crossed his arms over his chest, which ached for time lost. If he had been braver and taken action to act upon his feelings for Minerva sooner, they could have avoided years of misunderstandings.

He sat up and stared at his opponent. Camdon was seated in front of the white pieces, although he appeared to be in no rush to engage in another game, which was fine with Anthony. Kent had been right: he wasn't able to concentrate on the chessboard, not when, like Kent suspected, Minerva was about to embark upon a quest.

Kent returned to stand in front of the chessboard and glared down at him. "Do you have a clue as to what my sister might be planning?"

Anthony had an inkling, but he wasn't about to give up one of Minerva's secrets. "Not at this time." He leaned forward to rest his elbows on his knees. "Need I remind you, your sister warned me she will be playing to win, regardless of her feelings for me. She will not forfeit our game on purpose. Thus, I need to focus if I'm to win. The whole point of sequestering you two here was to help me develop a stratagem that even Minerva couldn't play her way out of. Now are you ready to assist me or not?"

Instead of reaching for a pawn to begin a new game, Camdon stood and faced Kent. "I don't think he has any idea how to go about defeating your sister. You best be prepared for the alternative."

Anthony stood to glare at Camdon. His friend might be a skilled agent for the Crown, but he was also an arrogant bastard, always underestimating others.

Ugh. Much like himself.

Camdon grabbed Kent's empty glass and walked over to the now half-empty decanter on the sideboard. He generously refilled the two glasses. "If Lady Minerva wins, what will the two of you do?"

In unison, Kent and Anthony replied, "Losing is not an option."

Ignoring Anthony, Camdon addressed Kent. "Aren't you even the least bit curious as to what your sister has planned, should she win?"

Kent answered, "Of course…and I've spent every waking hour trying to determine what my clever sister has devised. The problem is…"

Camdon grinned. "She's been planning for years, and you only have days. Perhaps our time would be better spent investigating what Minerva believes to be a more advantageous future than becoming Drake's wife."

"She wants to be more than a countess. She wants…" Kent placed his half-full drink back on the sideboard and marched toward the door. "I have an idea."

Anthony narrowed his gaze upon Kent. Had his friend figured out Minerva's secret plan? It wasn't likely, but he couldn't be certain.

Camdon followed Kent's lead and placed his empty glass back where it belonged, then turned to ask Anthony, "Are you coming?"

"Where exactly are you going?"

Kent answered, "Come along and find out."

Anthony's intuition told him to stay put. Trusting his instincts, he replied, "Not today."

Kent frowned. The disappointment in his gaze stabbed Anthony in his heart. Kent was more like a brother than friend. They had grown up inseparable, and for the majority of their lives they had always been in sync, or at least he had led Kent to believe so.

Camdon pushed Kent out into the foyer. "Leave him to study the board, and we shall make the necessary inquiries."

Anthony sat and peered through the open door until the booted footfalls of his friends faded into silence. Alone once more, a darkness settled about his heart. He turned back to face the black chess pieces in front of him. Normally he'd visualize the pieces shifting in his mind well before he physically moved them, but his mind remained blank.

He lifted his gaze to the empty seat opposite him. His imagination played a trick on him, projecting an image of Madame Rose in her velvety, low-cut, jewel-toned gown.

He blinked and Minerva appeared, dressed in a pale yellow dress styled in the same manner as the ones all the unmarried ladies wore.

Whom was he marrying?

Minerva wasn't only his best friend's sister that had grown up before his very eyes. There was this entirely mysterious side to the woman. He needed to better understand Minerva's alter ego.

He stood and turned away from the chessboard. If he could gain insight into this alternative life Minerva had planned, it might...just *might* be the key to figuring out how to win against her.

CHAPTER EIGHTEEN

ARMS SPREAD WIDE, Minerva twirled in the center of her rented room. And she sang…sang her favorite aria rather than having to hum it. Loud and clear. There was no need for her to escape into the gardens. Air filled her lungs and the notes escaped her, a little rusty but still freeing.

The walls shook. "Stop yer wailin'."

Her neighbors apparently were not theatre enthusiasts, at least not during the midday hours.

She spun around and scanned the room. It remained empty of furniture, but it was her space. Her heart filled with joy. She walked over to the window and peered out into the bustling street. The scene below was like a foreign land. Men and women moved about with purpose. No leisurely strolling. No one milling about waiting to be the first to witness a faux pas.

Minerva studied the women below and then glanced down at her bright yellow silk gown. Ugh. She would never blend in dressed like this. She tugged off her white gloves and marched to her trunk, which Jack had kindly brought up for her. Jack. It had taken her a good ten minutes to convince the footman to leave and not return for seventy-two hours. Three days of freedom to determine if becoming Madame Rose for a Season was truly the adventure she wished for before succumbing to the life of a spinster.

Minerva fell to her knees and opened the trunk. She threw blanket after blanket that she would later arrange into a makeshift bed next to her on the floor. It would be a far cry from her goose-down mattress that she had lain upon each night at Malbury Townhouse, but it would have to suffice for next two nights. She grabbed the subdued gray gown she'd managed to procure for such occasions and held it up to her chest. Giddy with excitement to join the crowd below, Minerva stood and brushed her skirts.

"Achoo." Dust tickled her nose.

She waited a moment, and when another sneeze failed to come, she let the gown fall back into the chest and reached behind her, ready to strip out of her dirty gown. She fumbled at the row of faux buttons, unable to release the clasps sewn into the material. Blast. She hadn't planned on being without her maid when she dressed this morn, and in her haste to leave, she had failed to change.

She slammed the trunk lid shut, irritated at her own lack of attention. She plonked down to sit upon the trunk and pressed her fingertips to her temples to think.

Minerva jumped at the scratch at the door. She wasn't expecting anyone.

No one was to know her whereabouts.

She tiptoed to the door and called out. "Who's there?"

"Tibby, me lady."

Lady. How did the stranger know she was a lady? Minerva stepped back from the door. Who in the blazes was Tibby, and what did she want?

"Me brother is Jack…yer footman. He sent me."

Minerva released the breath she had trapped in her lungs and opened the door with a whoosh. She came face to face with a fresh-faced woman who glared back at her. It was obvious Tibby was not at all pleased with her brother's orders.

Minerva grinned—she too disliked it when Benedict thought to order her about, even though the instances were few and far between.

Tibby's brow arched, and Minerva stepped back let the woman in. "You're Jack's sister?" She shut the door and leaned back against it. Jack had portrayed his little sister as a girl.

Tibby walked with determined steps to the window, muttering and inserting the occasional "tsk" now and then. Minerva wasn't dealing with a girl—no, Tibby was a young woman who carried herself with the maturity and confidence that came with years of experience at taking charge.

Tibby swiveled back around and marched with efficient steps to stand directly in front of Minerva. It was a good thing she blocked the door, for if Minerva had to guess, Tibby was not impressed with what she saw, including Minerva, and was ready to take her leave.

Hands on her hips, Tibby said, "Jack says I'm to assist ye. So…wot ye need 'elp with?"

"At present, getting out of this horrid gown."

If Minerva left her post at the door, would Tibby walk out? There was only one way to find out. Minerva pushed off the door and walked over to her trunk. She opened the lid and slid a sideways glance at Tibby, who was watching her every move with a critical eye. She withdrew the drab gown she wanted to wear and shook it out. "I think this might be more slightly more appropriate."

Tibby snorted. "Maybe if yer wantin' a job as a scullery maid or such." The young woman jutted her chin out toward the pile of blankets. "Ye plannin' to sleep upon those?"

Minerva nodded.

Tibby rolled her eyes to the ceiling, shook her head, and sighed. "I don't know wot me bleedin' brother is thinkin' leavin' ye 'ere with naught."

Minerva bristled at Tibby's words. "I have the funds to secure what I need. I simply want to—"

"Wot ye be needin' to do is return to Mayfair. That is what ye need." Tibby's brows knitted into a fierce scowl. "Ye 'ave no bloomin' clue wot's wot in this 'ere 'bouts." The brash woman reached out, turned Minerva by the shoulders, and made quick work of releasing the clasps. Then she stepped toward the door. "Is there anythin' else ye think ye need?"

Minerva gripped her gown to her chest and answered, "No." She willed her chin not to quiver. No one had ever spoken to her so directly before, or with so little care.

Tibby took one more glance about the room. "Grand, cuz I've not got time to be pandering to a lady who is unappreciative of wot ye got."

In a blink, the girl was gone.

Tears welled in Minerva's eyes and spilled over her cheeks. She caught her pitiful reflection in the window. Bah. She was no watering pot. And she certainly wasn't one to wallow in self-pity.

She let her silk gown drop to the ground and grabbed the cotton dress she intended to venture out in. Minerva tugged the material over her head and tied the sash behind her back with brisk efficiency. Tibby was wrong. She may be a daughter of an earl, but her life wasn't all pleasure and leisure.

Minerva returned to the chest, fished out her coin purse and retrieved two crowns, and tucked them into the sewn-in pockets. She wasn't about to let Tibby's comments spoil her plans.

THE HEELS OF her feet were blistered, and the abundance of energy she normally possessed was depleted. Minerva hugged the white square of linen that housed two bruised apples, a loaf of bread, and a chunk of cheese—all questionably edible at best— tight to her chest. She wasn't about to be robbed of her possessions a second time, not when she was close to making it back safely to the stairs that led up to her rooms.

How quickly her confidence had diminished once she realized that the urchins she had given apples to were the very same ones who had pushed and tripped her to gain her basket full of food.

Tibby's words rattled through her thoughts and once again ignited enough anger to dry up her tears and push her to try again. She'd woefully underestimated the resilience needed to be self-sufficient, but she wasn't one to give up easily.

Her hip ached as she mounted the steps to her rooms. To her sanctuary. She made it to the third step before a shooting pain radiated from the bottom of her feet up her tired legs and lodged in her chest. Minerva was left winded, grasping for the handrail and unable to move. Her chin dropped to her chest and she closed her eyes. *Keep moving,* her mind screamed, but her body refused to respond. Tibby was correct—she was a pampered lady who couldn't even manage to obtain the basic necessities. A droplet escaped from the corner of her eye and trickled down her cheek.

No more tears.

She heaved in a deep breath and rocked herself forward to mount the remaining few steps and then trudge down the landing. Breathless, she stood in front of the door that only hours ago represented endless opportunities, but now appeared as worn as she felt. She rested her forehead against the door. Voices from within had her straightening and pressing an ear to the wood.

"No, no, no, not there, you dunderhead." It was Tibby's direct, cutting voice. "Over there in the corner, behind the blasted privacy screen."

Minerva pushed open the unlocked door. How in the blazes had Tibby gained entrance?

Her gaze fell to the hairpin still lodged in the lock. Apparently, Tibby was not only good at directing people about—she was also skilled at picking locks.

Minerva glanced about the room and nearly lost the bundle in her arms. Curtains blocked out the dwindling sunlight, but she could make out the settee littered with cushions, the small table and two chairs placed near the widow, and a great hulk of a man placing a small table and basin in the corner.

"Lady Minerva!" Tibby exclaimed. "Gawd, what the devil

happened to you?" Jack's sister rushed to her side and ushered her to sit on the settee. Tibby reached for the food, but Minerva pulled back. She wasn't ready to relinquish her treasure just quite yet.

Tibby left her on the settee. The splashing of water snapped Minerva out of her mild trance. Tibby poured water into a basin and brought it back with her, settling it on the small table next to the settee. A handkerchief mysteriously appeared, and Tibby dipped the clean white material into the water and wrung it out. "Yer a mess, me lady." The young woman ran the cool cloth over Minerva's forehead and cheeks. Tibby moved with sure, methodical movements. "I need to take a look at yer hands." She reached out, took the bundle out of Minerva's arms, and placed it on the settee. Minerva held out her hands, and Tibby turned them over, palms up.

The woman blinked and then muttered, "Tsk-tsk." Then she removed Minerva's bloodstained kid gloves.

Minerva tried not to wince, but the stinging sensation was hard to disregard.

Twisted at the waist, Tibby dipped the handkerchief into the water once more before she set to work cleaning Minerva's palms. "Wot ye got in there? 'ad best be worth it." She glanced at the parcel and then back at Minerva. "Did ye hurt yer knees too?" Without waiting for a reply, Tibby lifted Minerva's skirts and examined her knees. She shook her head and again uttered a series of disapproving tsks. Tibby continued with practiced precision, cleaning the scrapes and bruises.

The silence got to Minerva first, and she asked, "Why did you come back?" She scanned the room that was bare no longer.

"I went home, and me mam reminded me of yer constant generosity. Reminded me it was cuz of ye and yer bloomin' bonuses ye give Jack that I'm not havin' to..." Tibby looked up. "Umm...ye best not ask what exactly me mam's words were." Boots shuffled behind them, and Tibby looked over her shoulder. "Stop starin' at the lady and go fetch the bleedin' cupboard and bring it up."

She dropped Minerva's skirts, causing Minerva to hiss as the material rubbed against her raw, albeit now clean, skin.

"Yer knees should 'eal nice and quick. But…" Tibby picked up Minerva's hands and reexamined them. "Yer hands are gonna take some time to 'eal."

Minerva groaned. She'd have to wear gloves for her match with Anthony. "Would honey help them heal faster? Gregory always puts honey on our cuts and scrapes."

Tibby frowned at her. "Does he?"

Minerva nodded.

"Then I'll bring yer some tomorrow."

Minerva waited for Tibby's attention to return. She'd seen the all-too-familiar glazed look on Gregory's features too often to know better than to try to attempt to converse with a healer sorting through the advantages and disadvantages of a new treatment.

When Tibby's gaze cleared, Minerva said, "My thanks for your assistance. I really do appreciate it, but I must ask, did anyone see or follow you here?"

"Jack didn't say ye were in hidin'." Tibby frowned.

Minerva let out a humorless chuckle. "I thought it would be a lark to be someone, anyone but myself, for a spell."

Tibby snorted at her dream. "And who were ye wanting to be?"

"Madame Rose." Minerva smirked at Tibby's large eyes. "Just for a Season."

Tibby's gaze fell to her bosom, which was discreetly tucked away. "Ye've got to be funning me." Tibby scanned Minerva's features. "Yer Madame Rose?"

Minerva nodded. "You have heard of her?"

"Ye gads. Of course I 'ave. Every-bloomin'-one has heard of Madame Rose." Tibby rose and took the basin and the now pink-stained water to the window. She pushed the glass pane open with the barest of nudges of her elbow and then tipped the water out without a care if anyone was below.

Since there were no shouts from the street, Minerva smiled and held her tongue. She couldn't read the girl. What did Tibby think of Madame Rose?

Tibby put the basin back upon the table in the corner and went to open the door, and in came the brute of a man, all sweaty and with a cupboard strapped to his back. "Where ye be wantin' this one?"

Minerva had excellent hearing, yet she'd not noticed any loud grunts or footfalls from the giant hauling the furniture into her room.

Tibby pointed and said, "Next to the door."

The man straightened and placed the large piece of furniture exactly where Tibby had instructed. The young woman then picked up Minerva's spoils of the day and tossed the man an apple. "Me thanks, Grant. I'll be lookin' on Maci as soon as I'm done 'ere."

Minerva waited for the man to leave and then said, "You're a healer."

"Wot if I am?"

"It's no wonder you are so bossy." Minerva grinned. "Just like my brother Gregory."

Tibby turned. "He's the one studying to be a physician, is he not?"

"He is."

With a shake of her head, Tibby went to a small box set upon the small dining table. She pulled out a set of plates, cups, saucers, and a teapot, and carefully placed them inside the cabinet. "It's not much, but ye've got enough to survive for the short respite you wished for." Staring at Minerva, Tibby tilted her head and smiled. "Never in a thousand years would I have guessed ye were Madame Rose." Still in a state of disbelief, she shook her head, grabbed her cloak, and headed for the door.

Minerva called out, "Will you be back?"

"Wot ye want now?" Tibby turned and stared at Minerva.

Forcing her lips to curve into a fake smile, Minerva replied, "Nothing. I was simply making an inquiry." Wandering the streets this afternoon had taught Minerva a lesson she'd not forget anytime soon—you could be all alone even when surrounded by many.

"I'll be back." Tibby closed the door and then popped her head back in. "I'll bring ye some honey and a kettle for tea."

Minerva rested her head back and sighed, exhausted from her emotions continuously volleying from highs to lows over the past few days. She had prided herself on her keen ability to adapt, yet faced with the realities of an entirely new social system, Minerva found herself more confused and undecided.

She looked about the room. None of it was gilded, but it was functional. She'd never backed down from a challenge, and she wasn't going to start now. She had days to learn how to maneuver within her new setting. It was a challenge she both wanted and feared.

CHAPTER NINETEEN

THE GEL HE had been trailing for the past three hours was running Anthony ragged. As day turned into night, he shortened the distance he maintained to keep out of sight, but the young woman was astute, always checking her surroundings for threats. Who was she?

This whole debacle began when he had snuck into Minerva's rooms at the Malbury townhouse and confirmed she was indeed missing. To his surprise, he also noted Minerva's most trusted footman, Jack, was going about his daily duties as if nothing was amiss. Jack was no ordinary footman. No, the man was Minerva's personal guard. Which raised the question, why the devil was he not with Minerva?

Anthony had hidden in the gardens to watch the back service entrance for some clue as to where or how he'd be able to track Minerva down. Legs cramped, he'd been ready to give up when the slight young gel, hood pulled down to cover her features, appeared and summoned Jack. Her back was to him, so Anthony could only read Jack's lips and caught half of the conversation, which was not entirely helpful, since the footman was adept at covert communications. Whatever information the woman was sharing, Jack appeared displeased with it.

Trusting his intuition, Anthony had left his post in the gardens and followed the woman, who was still leading him to and fro about Town. With each passing hour, his hope that Jack's visitor would lead him to Minerva dwindled.

He tipped his hat lower as they left Mayfair and entered King's Square. It mattered not whose door the woman rapped on; she was always admitted with swift, eager anticipation. Deciphering the reason for her visits kept Anthony preoccupied while he waited for her to reappear. However, with each residence they visited, the possibilities for her gallivanting all over London increased rather than narrowed.

Lost in thought, he nearly lost sight of his target as she ducked into another side alley.

He quickened his pace as he wandered through King's Square.

King's Square.

Anthony froze in his tracks. King's Square sat in between Mayfair and the artisan district that housed art studios, playhouses, galleries…and the theatre. What a dunderhead he'd been following the gel all afternoon, when he should have headed for Wembley Hall and begun his investigations there. Damn woman.

Anthony swiveled and took off in the opposite direction. An image of Minerva disguised as Madame Rose flashed before him. His heart raced. Not from the fact that he'd begun to jog, but from the memory of his kiss with Madame Rose. The kiss that had haunted his dreams and plagued his thoughts daily for years, evoking guilt and pleasure that he couldn't dispel.

Whom was he really searching for, Minerva or Madame Rose? It mattered not, for he was in love with both of them. He simply wanted to hold the woman and convince her of how much he adored her…how much she meant to him…how a life with him could be more fulfilling than the life of an actress. He'd have to solidify his arguments to persuade her, but he was determined.

Thirty minutes later, parched and sweaty, Anthony leaned back against the cool stone wall that afforded him a clear view of the back entrance to Wembley Hall. What an idiot, wasting all those hours following a hunch born out of desperation. He heaved in a deep breath. Clarity of mind and a steady pulse were what he needed. There wasn't any sign of Minerva, but he still believed she was close, or his nerves would never have calmed.

After continuously scanning the alley and the steady stream of pedestrians, Anthony finally spotted the gel he had trailed earlier. Damn, had she detected him earlier and waited until she was sure he was no longer following her? Clever chit. His assessment of the woman was further confirmed when she slowed her pace and scanned the area with narrowed eyes before mounting a set of stairs to the upper floors. He raised his gaze to catch a glimpse of who opened the door, but the angle was all wrong. Eyes closed, he concentrated and tuned out the bustle of the street.

"Oh, Tibby, you're back." A singsong voice filled with relief floated down. It wasn't Minerva's usual no-nonsense, direct tone, but it was definitely her.

"Madame Rose…" There was a questioning quality to the girl's response.

Anthony peered up at the empty landing. He'd have to wait for the gel, Tibby, to leave before he could go up and reacquaint himself with Madame Rose.

He shook his head. He'd known Minerva for better than half of his life; he should have seen the woman beneath the face paint. Mayhap he had on a certain level. Was it possible that his subconscious knew, and that was why he had ventured to dally with the actress when he'd not been tempted to lie with a woman in years?

The creak of a door brought his attention back to up to the landing where Tibby had disappeared from. The gel stealthily slipped out of the room and descended the stairs, scanning the area multiple times. He stepped back out of sight and held his breath. After the count of sixty, he slowly released the breath and peeked back at the alley. With no sign of the gel about, he stepped out and marched up the stairs.

Knuckles raised to rap on the wood door, Anthony was stunned as the door flung open and he came face to face with the woman who was to be his future countess, who was currently taking on the appearance of Madame Rose. He stared at her. And the truth hit him. She was more than an actress…more than a lady. She wasn't a woman to be pegged for a single role. She was a woman who could become anyone she wanted to be.

With a new perspective on what he suspected was Minerva's true wish for the future, he let his arm fall to his side. He opened his mouth to say… What had he come here to say? What the blazes was wrong with him, staring at Minerva like she was a stranger?

With the door held slightly ajar, Minerva peered at him and said, "Lord Drake."

"Madame Rose." He attempted to keep his gaze trained on her face, but it trailed down her elegant neck to the exposed tops of her breasts that were threatening to topple out of her low-cut gown. With a nod, he asked, "Are you going to invite me in, Minerva, or keep me waiting?"

Minerva took a step back and waved him in with the flair and attitude of a seasoned actress. "I suppose I shouldn't be surprised you tracked me down."

"Trust me, it wasn't easy. I nearly wore a hole in my boots trailing the woman you referred to as Tibby."

Shocked, Minerva replied, "But Tibby swore she lost you nearly three-quarters of an hour ago."

"The gel did." He spun around in a slow circle. "Why are you here?" How in the blazes had she managed to maintain a separate residence all these years without his knowledge?

"I could ask the same of you." Minerva played with the end of the silk sash that was loosely bound about her waist.

He took in her painted face and glared at the faux beauty mark and the lush pink lips that all the gentlemen at White's wrote poems over on the rare occasions she supposedly crossed the channel and sang for them. Except the woman before him had never had to endure the rolling waves to reach English soil. No. Minerva simply had to devise a plan that allowed her the freedom to don her alter ego on the rare night she was able to pull off the ruse.

"Remind me, what excuse did you use the last time you ventured out as Madame Rose?"

"That was two years ago, my lord. I don't recall."

It was true: Madame Rose hadn't reappeared after their kiss. Not that he'd wanted to ever lay eyes on the woman who had tempted him beyond the pale and made him feel like he was being unfaithful to Minerva.

Fists clenched at his sides, Anthony said, "I can't believe you tricked me into kissing you."

"I did no such thing." She stomped over to the sofa and sat primly like the lady she was. "It's not my fault you simply wanted to kiss Madame Rose and not me."

"You and Madame Rose are one and the same!"

"Are we?" Minerva leaned back and settled herself against the plush cushions. "If you had kissed me when I was dressed as your best friend's sister, you might have found out that the woman you had been running from all these years was actually the same woman you nearly...nearly seduced." Her silk robe slipped from her shoulder as she shrugged. "Why did you come here?"

He crossed the small room in a few strides and loomed over Minerva, who refused to meet his gaze. His unsated desire for Madame Rose vanished into thin air. He didn't want Madame Rose; he wanted Minerva.

He blinked at his own confusion and sank down to sit on the end of the settee. "I came here to..." He raised his hand and squeezed the back of his neck. Why the blazes *had* he come? He hung his head and rubbed his temples. "If I lose, and you win our match, this...this is the life you wish to lead?"

"Yes."

He rose to stand. "Are you certain you want to live like"—he waved his arm and did a half-turn before returning his gaze to her—"this?"

She raised her chin and met his gaze directly. "Yes."

"You would rather be Madame Rose than become the Countess of Drake." His statement left a sour taste upon his tongue. He wanted her to denounce his claim, prove he was right that it wasn't about merely taking on the role as Madame Rose for a Season—it was the freedom it gave her.

He sank down beside her on the settee. Minerva reached for his hand and shifted to face him. Egad. Had he been wrong?

He squeezed her hand, prompting her to speak her mind.

Minerva rolled her shoulders back and said, "You are a peer. A gentleman. You don't understand."

"Explain it to me." If his scheme to win succeeded, they needed to be able to communicate openly and honestly with one another, rather than keeping their fears to themselves, as they had in the past.

"Very well." She had dropped the singsong lilt to her voice and returned to her no-nonsense, direct speech. "It's not that I don't want to be your wife, it's that I…I want to win, so that I may gain my freedom to be Madame Rose. The freedom to…" She snapped her mouth closed and lowered her gaze to her lap.

He wanted to confess that he understood, but they needed to have the conversation so they both fully understood the stakes of their match. If she was to become his wife, she needed to trust him, to believe she could share her deepest desires and dreams.

He ran his thumb over her knuckles. "Freedom to do what?"

"To experience life." She lifted her gaze to him. Eyes bright with hope, she continued, "I want the freedom to be more than the daughter of an earl."

They were making progress. He wanted to see her smile. "So…what you are telling me is that you want the choice to take on any role that might capture your fancy. Pirate, explorer, or even…" Her needlepoint was atrocious and her least favorite endeavor, so he added, "Dressmaker."

Minerva granted him his wish—she grinned at him and replied, "Yes and no. Yes, I want to do whatever it is that captures my interest…" A flare of desire burned bright in her gaze. "I want the option to pursue adventures here close to my family and…" Minerva released his hand and stood. She meandered to the window and peered down. Barely louder than a whisper, she added, "I want to experience what a spinster can only dream of."

Damn the minx. She wasn't fantasizing about sailing the seas; she was alluding to the intimacies between a man and a woman. He shot to his feet and strode to stand behind her. "What do spinsters dream of?" He already knew the answer, but would she be daring enough to say it, to demand it?

She turned. The moonlight fell upon her flushed cheeks that even face paint could not hide. "Of taking a lover and never being caught." Minerva wrapped her arms around his neck and guided his head down to her.

One kiss. He'd grant her one kiss.

Wrapped in his arms, her lush form pressed against him, igniting every nerve in his body. She made him feel full of life. Invincible. Desired.

One of her petite hands left the back of his neck and trailed down his chest between them, and then lower to cup his engorged manhood. Her bold touches had him acting on instinct. He released the clasps at the back of her gown and eased the material down until it pooled at her feet. He skimmed his palm over her bare bottom and then gave her a good smack.

She froze and stared up at him. With a smirk she ran her thumb along the full length of him trapped in his pants up to the tip, and then flicked the sensitive head with her finger. A groan escaped him. She was a quick learner, and, as a chess master, she would match his every move.

He bent and scooped her up in his arms, and her silk stockings caressed his forearms. Five quick, long strides and they were back next to the settee. He should take her to bed, tuck her in, and leave. But he didn't trust himself to go anywhere near a bed, not when he had so little self-control left.

Minerva glanced over his shoulder at her bed. He ignored her unspoken plea and sat on the settee and adjusted her on his lap. His cock ached as her bottom slid against it.

"Do you intend to win our match?" she asked.

"I do."

She leaned in closer. "Then if you win—"

He didn't let her finish. "There is no if. I will win."

Lips aligned with his, Minerva poked her tongue out over her bottom lip. He wanted to devour her mouth and suck on her tongue like he had two years ago. She hadn't forgotten. But the minx was playing a dangerous game. He had little, if any, self-control to speak of.

She guided his head down to speak into his ear. "If you are certain, then there is no harm if we indulge tonight."

His muddled brain followed her logic. Honor would dictate he refuse her offer and wait until he had won before taking her innocence.

Minerva's nimble fingers had worked the buttons of both his jacket and waistcoat free. Without hesitation, he stripped out of the garments and his lawn shirt. He wanted to feel her skin next to his. He'd refrained two years ago and regretted it every day since. He wasn't one to repeat mistakes.

Mid-stroke down her thigh, his hand froze. What if he lost?

Minerva trailed kisses along his neck and then his shoulder, sending a tingling sensation down his spine and firing every cell below his waist. Blood pooled in his loins.

"Drake, take me to bed," she whispered, nipping at his ear.

He caved. Anthony lifted her into his arms and took her to bed. He sat her on the edge, and she promptly went to work on the buttons of his pants.

He gripped her wrist. "Are you certain this is what you want?"

"I have no doubt."

There was a twinkle in her eye and a slight hitch in her breath before she uttered the word *doubt*. Was it his conscience warning him not to proceed, or was it nerves on Minerva's part? She was an innocent—a well-educated innocent, but an innocent all the same.

He released her, and she pushed his pants down to the floor. She was mirroring his earlier moves. Smart minx. He'd have to go slow or he might find himself unable to control his baser needs.

Minerva scooted back and tucked her legs under her so she ended up facing him and kneeling in the middle of the bed. She placed her hands behind her. Did she know of his preferences?

She peered up at him. No. Minerva was acting on pure instinct. If she was aware of his partiality for vigorous bed sport, she'd have not been brazen enough to suggest taking her maiden head before they wed.

"You're too far away, pet," he said. "Come back and sit on the edge in front of me."

Minerva didn't hesitate. Her silk-clad legs dangled over the edge of the bed. He sank to his knees and spread her legs wide to accommodate his shoulders. Eyes locked with hers, he gave her a wink and then wedged his head firmly between her thighs and darted his tongue out to glide over her core. Her unique scent and taste burned into his memory.

Her fingers dug into his shoulders as he laved over her slit until he found the sensitive nub that he oh so enjoyed teasing. Minerva's moans were increasing in volume. He slid a finger into her tight, untried channel. She was wet and ready for him.

He rolled back and stood. Instead of scooting back like before, Minerva stared down at his erect manhood and slid off the bed. Her gaze met his as she grabbed his cock at the base and began to tentatively pleasure him with her mouth. Move for move.

His cock already slick from her deep kisses, Anthony placed his hand over hers and guided it to stroke him from the tip down to the base and back with firm pressure. Her hand slid easily back and forth until he could bear it no more. He wanted to be buried deep inside Minerva.

"It's time." He pulled back, and his hard cock slid out of her mouth with a pop. "On the bed."

Minerva rose and turned, and her butt brushed against his cock. He resisted the temptation to push her against the bed and take her from behind. It was her first experience, so he needed to go slow, not hard and fast. But he failed to resist the invitation to swat her bottom as she crawled up onto the bed.

She twisted to look back at him. Instead of a rebuff, Minerva gave him a wink and wiggled her bottom. He refrained. She would one day, once she was his wife, learn the consequences for asking for more.

He followed her up onto the bed and settled on his side next to the future Countess Drake. What should his next move be, knowing the minx would do something equally devilish to him?

Various options flashed through his mind. Before he could decide, Minerva took matters into her own hands and wiggled her way beneath him and spread her legs. Positioned to drive into her, he exerted the last remnants of control and kissed her until the tip of his cock was coated with her moisture.

"Ready?"

Minerva stared back at him and nodded.

He thrust forward. Damn. The minx was untried and tight. The pleasure drove him forward until he was buried deep.

Slow. Go. Slow.

With utter control, he brought Minerva to a climax, thrusting slow and deep. She clawed at his shoulders, and he spilled his seed into her.

Exhausted and out of breath, he rolled onto the bed and lay on his back, but he missed the feeling of her body against him. He shifted onto his side, mirroring Minerva's position. She was faced away from him, but as soon as he rolled over, she had snuggled into him until her back was up against his chest. He draped an arm around her waist and closed his eyes.

Minerva was his...forever.

FEELING OVERLY WARM, Minerva threw off the blankets. Sunlight warmed her skin, and she reluctantly opened her eyes.

She wasn't in her chambers. The makeshift curtains only partially blocked out the daylight.

She blinked and rubbed her eyes. She was Madame Rose and abed with Anthony. Minerva stared at the naked man next to her. He was mumbling in his sleep. She leaned down closer to decipher what Anthony was saying. A mistake, for the first words she recognized were "Madame Rose." He was fantasizing about her alter ego.

A burst of anger rolled through her, which was utterly senseless, since she *was* Madame Rose.

What the devil was wrong with her?

It should matter not if Anthony uttered "Minerva" or "Madame Rose"—she was one and the same. Yet if she was Madame Rose, then the consequences for her actions last night would not entail her meeting Anthony at the altar. As Madame Rose, she could take on lovers and need not give up her independence. Not that she wanted anyone but Anthony as a lover, but if she could retain her freedom and still enjoy his company in the evenings, she would have the best of both her worlds.

She flopped back on to the bed.

The movement had Anthony opening his eyes and smiling. "A good morn to you."

"Yes, a very good morning to you too." Minerva rolled off the bed and stood looking about for her silk robe. Not spying it anywhere, she trudged over to her trunk to find it.

"What are you searching for?" Anthony asked, sitting up barechested with the bed linens covering his lower half. The half that she now had intimate knowledge of.

She ducked her head so he wouldn't see her grin. "My robe." The silky material brushed against her fingertips, and she retrieved the garment. She stood, looped her arms through the holes, and tied the sash securely around her waist.

When she turned to face the bed, she was disappointed to see Anthony had left the bed and was already half-dressed with his pants and lawn shirt on.

Minerva put her hands on her hips and asked, "Leaving?"

"Since you were donning clothes, I thought I'd do the same."

Hm. The downfalls of loving someone who matched your every move. Although countering his every move and his doing the same had proven rather enjoyable in bed.

She glanced at the bed and then back to Anthony. To spend the day abed with him would be decadent. But her time as Madame Rose was limited, especially if he were to win their game.

She bridged the space between them and said, "Probably for the best. Shouldn't you be at home strategizing with my brother and Lord Camdon?"

Eyes wide, he ceased fiddling with his buttons. "You're not intending to play to win. Are you?"

She buttoned up his waistcoat. "I always play to win." Minerva stepped back and clasped her hands behind her back. The temptation to undo her handiwork and return to bed with Anthony was becoming all too alluring.

"But last night—"

"Last night proved to be thoroughly enjoyable and extremely enlightening. Let me remind you, as Madame Rose, I'm free to do as I please."

He loomed over her. "Let me remind you, Lady Minerva Malbury, that after what transpired between us in that bed, you are mine...forever." Anthony didn't wait for a response; he simply turned on his heel and marched out her door, grumbling about having to wait another day or two to claim her as his wife.

Her knees had literally weakened at his declaration. She loved the demanding, exacting side of his personality, because he never revealed that aspect of his character to anyone but her, not even her brother Benedict.

Anthony's parting words replayed in her mind. What if he did win?

She recalled his steely, determined glare. A shiver of panic ran down her back.

There was no time to waste. She walked over to the window and looked down at the bustling street below. If Anthony won, she had but two more days of freedom as Madame Rose.

She marched back to her trunk and extracted a low-cut, deep burgundy gown that no unmarried lady would be allowed to wear in public.

Madame Rose was about to go on an adventure.

CHAPTER TWENTY

MALE VOICES FLOATED through the halls as Anthony entered his townhome. He marched down to his study, where he found Kent and Camdon lounging in the chairs facing the dying embers in the fireplace. Each held a tumbler filled with liquid that glowed a golden amber. He wasn't sure if the rage flowing through his veins was due to the men helping themselves to his private whisky collection or the fact that Minerva had once again correctly predicted the movements of those close to them.

He ignored his friends, walked over to stand next to the chessboard, and stared at the pieces. Minerva often equated life to a game of chess. Except in his experience, not everyone played by the same set of rules in real life.

Camdon slapped a hand on his shoulder and asked, "Where the devil have you been?"

"Out."

"Out visiting your mistress?"

Heat and anger rolled through Anthony at his friend's unknowing inference to Minerva as a mistress. He frowned and replied, "I don't have one at present."

Kent joined them and raised his glass in the air in the direction of Anthony's jawline. "Then explain how you obtained those smudges of white face paint near your ear?"

Anthony had no intention of answering Kent's question, or he might be meeting his best friend at dawn in a muddy field somewhere. He pulled out the chair in front of the chessboard and sank into it. "I need to prepare for my match with your sister."

Nonplussed by his change of topic, Camdon promptly sank into the chair opposite him and began to arrange the pieces in front of him so that they were centered within their square. The man was meticulous.

"Did the two of you discover any more information regarding Minerva's plans?"

Camdon sat back and grumbled, "Every idea, every lead, led us back here."

"Here, as in my residence?"

"Yes." Kent chuckled. "Knowing Minerva, she's hatched numerous plans and laid some decoys related to her scheme at large. But wouldn't it be a lark to find out that her ultimate plan all along was to become the Countess of Drake?"

Was Kent correct? Had the minx somehow planned *all* of this?

Arms crossed over his chest, Anthony stared at the wood pieces in front of him. The hours he'd spent with Minerva replayed in his mind on a continuous loop. His heart sank every time he remembered the excruciating pleasure he experienced as he released his seed in her. He'd been careless. What if she became enceinte and died? It would be all his fault.

Mayhap the possibility of Minerva winning was a good thing. For he might be the death of her. Last night proved he'd not be able to refrain from venturing to her bed once they were married. He had no self-control when it came to Minerva.

"The pieces shan't move by themselves," Kent prompted as he dragged another chair over to join them. "Any luck devising a strategy to defeat Minerva?"

A seedling of doubt started to sprout. It was conceivable Anthony could lose, but should he forfeit? Minerva had made it abundantly clear earlier that she believed assuming the role of

Madame Rose was far more favorable than becoming the next Countess of Drake, even after spending the night abed with him.

Anthony glanced up at Kent. "Your sister's moves are highly unpredictable. I'd be a fool to believe I could concoct a solitary strategy that would see me crowned the winner."

"Then…predict the unpredictable," Camdon said as he swiveled the board around until the white pieces were again in front of him. Why bother moving the board only to place it back in its original position?

With a frown, Camdon sat back in his seat, closed his eyes, and pinched the bridge of his nose. "After following one fruitless lead after another, I've come to the realization that Lady Minerva's chess play is much like how she conducts her clandestine activities."

Anthony was well aware that Camdon's statement was accurate—however, it might prove helpful to gain the perspective of a spy. "How so?"

Camdon opened his eyes and stared down at the pieces on the board. "It was during our investigation that I began to recognize a pattern. As we gained each piece of information, our confidence in success grew. Much like when I captured each of Minerva's pieces during our match, my belief in defeating the clever chit amplified." He moved the pieces in front of him, replaying the first four moves of his game with Minerva, and then continued, "But what I failed to realize during our game was that with each move, I too was providing critical information that increased Minerva's odds of winning."

"Do you suspect Minerva was tracking your progress?"

"Doubtful. My instincts tell me that the wild goose chase was merely a diversion. Instead of following the clues, we should have looked to do the opposite. Except we were able to discover she had been sighted in and about King's Square, which then led to evidence that she had returned to Mayfair, which we now know to be untrue." Camdon continued to play out the moves, pausing each time he replicated one of Minerva's. He peered up at

Anthony. "All morn I've been wondering, why lead us to King's Square?"

"How many clues did it take you before you found yourself in King's Square?"

Kent gazed into his glass and then answered, "Eight hours, and sixteen clues."

Anthony pondered. Was that Minerva's prediction—that she'd defeat him in eight hours or in sixteen moves? He continued to observe Camdon moving the pieces in front of them.

The combination of her moves struck Anthony. It was like she wanted her opponent to win, but her pride would not allow her to forfeit the game. He leaned forward to study the board closer. She had sacrificed her queen, which represented her alter ego, Madame Rose. Anthony sharply sat back in his chair.

With a smirk, Camdon said, "You know where she is, don't you?"

Anthony was a terrible liar, so he hedged his answer. "Mayhap."

Kent rose to his feet and demanded, "Where?"

Anthony *should* tell his best friend where his wayward sister was. But Minerva wanted independence. And she had proven over the years that she wasn't in need of the protection he or her brother could provide.

"I merely want to ensure she is happy and safe."

Anthony glanced up at Kent, who was disheveled and with dark smudges under his eyes. The man was clearly worried, and so Anthony replied, "Do you think I'd be here if I thought that she was in harm's way?"

"I no longer know what to think about your actions. None of which make any sense to me and haven't since…since I married." Kent slumped back into his chair.

"I've heard getting one's leg shackled changes a man's perspective," Camdon chimed in, and rose, taking the glass that was close to shattering from Kent's hand. "I'll pour us another."

Kent bowed his head and said, "You realize we were idiots.

We should have been more honest with the women we loved, and with each other."

"Even if you hadn't objected to my pursuing Minerva, I wouldn't doom her to a life without children," Anthony said.

"You are an imbecile." Kent stared him with eyes that appeared wiser than Anthony remembered his best friend possessing.

The verbal slight meant little between them. It was the anguish in Kent's eyes that had Anthony slouching in his chair. "Minerva no longer wishes to become the Countess of Drake, and after consideration, I can't fault her for desiring the alternative life she has planned."

"That's because the two of you think too much alike. I can hardly fathom a life better than being with the person...the woman who makes you whole. A lady who accepts you for all your faults and loves you in spite of them." Kent took the glass Camdon held out for him.

Camdon resumed his seat and added, "I've not known Minerva long, but I doubt whatever life she has conceived could hold her interest for more than a summer."

"Whatever led you to that belief?" Anthony asked.

"Think about it. Objectively. Minerva loves her siblings first and foremost. It won't take Chestwick long to get his lady's belly full. I suspect Minerva wouldn't miss the birth of her nephew or niece for anything or whatever life you believe she wishes. Even if she wins your match, Minerva will not abandon her family."

Camdon's logic was sound, but it changed nothing. Minerva had no intentions of forfeiting the game, and Anthony was beginning to doubt whether he had the fortitude to refrain from touching her again should he win, which would ultimately result in her death. French letters were not fail-proof.

"I want to see for myself she is safe. Tell me where I can find her," Kent pleaded.

"Do you trust me?" Anthony asked.

Kent hesitated, when he never had before. "Of course."

"Then trust that I'll ensure she remains safe until she returns to Malbury Townhouse."

Kent placed the half-full glass next to the chessboard. "Very well. I'm off to track down Phyllis and beg her for forgiveness."

"For?"

"My idiotic behavior." He stormed out of the room at a near run.

Camdon chuckled. "Kent's a lucky man to have found a woman as understanding as Phyllis."

"It's not so much that Phyllis is an understanding lady; it's more that they understand each other."

Camdon's brow arched. "How very insightful of you." He lifted his glass and gulped down the quarter-century-aged whisky then placed his empty glass upon the table next to the fallen queen. "You should plan on attending Penwort's ball this eve." Camdon reached for Kent's tumbler and finished it off as well. "I shall be aboard a slip headed for the south of Spain."

"Assigned to leave already?"

With a nod and a chuckle, Camdon said, "My punishment for failing my mission."

Anthony was saddened to hear his friend was leaving. Being away from home and family, he imagined, was a lonely existence. "The odds of your defeating Minerva were slim. How unjust."

"Regardless, I failed. I hope you shall not do the same." Camdon bowed and headed out the door.

"When will you return?" Anthony asked his dejected friend.

Camdon turned and said, "The penalty is a fairly easy assignment. I hope to be back in time to witness you utter your vows."

"You're confident I shall win."

"I have no doubt you are more than capable. The real question is, what will you choose—to love Minerva as husband or to remain her friend?" Camdon shook his head as he headed out.

Anthony stared at the chess pieces. The was no choice. He wanted Minerva as wife.

CHAPTER TWENTY-ONE

WITH HER BACK up against the wall, Minerva let her head fall forward and sighed. She cradled her injured left hand in her right. After spending an inordinate amount of time building and lighting a fire, she'd quickly discovered how ill-prepared she was to complete even the simplest of tasks, like boiling water for a cup of tea.

She squeezed her eyes shut. The burning throb of pain at the center of her palm was nothing compared to the ache deep in her chest that grew every hour she spent alone. She had scoffed at Anthony's lack of will to remain hidden, and even laughed at the fact it had only taken two days of solitary confinement for the man to come to his senses. How vain of her to consider she would fare better than Anthony. She hadn't even been left alone for more than a day and she already missed everyone, but especially the man she had lain with willingly in her makeshift bed.

Overconfident in her abilities, she had once again ventured out only to find herself lost amongst a sea of people. It was a peculiar sensation to be surrounded by others and yet feel entirely isolated. The street vendors that were usually attentive and friendly behaved as if she were invisible. Dressed as Madame Rose, she was treated with apathy rather than enthusiasm.

With near-perfect hearing, she couldn't ignore the snide

references to her being some poor pigeon's mistress or the pitying looks from others. Evidently it mattered not if she was Madame Rose or Lady Minerva—people gossiped about her or pitied her regardless.

Humiliated, she'd returned to her rooms hoping a cup of tea would restore her spirits. When she walked through her door and found herself all alone, she clutched at her chest, the pain so intense it caused her to gasp for a breath. The ache wasn't due to the fact she had no one to order about. It wasn't the knowledge that her family had moved on without her. And it definitely wasn't the fact that she missed the comforts of being a lady.

No, the pain was all due to the realization that what she truly desired was to continue being Lady Minerva Malbury, surrounded by her siblings and close friends, all of whom she could trust. She didn't want to be anyone else. The fantasy of living as Madame Rose, with loving and adoring supporters all about her, had been demolished. Assuming the identity of her alter ego for a Season wasn't going to make her happy. She needed to be a part of her siblings' lives, mayhap not in the role of mother any longer, but in other ways.

A sharp rap at the door had Minerva scurrying over to the exit.

She pressed her ear to the door. "Who's there?"

"It's me. Tibby."

The prospect of having company had Minerva clumsily turning the latch with her good hand and fumbling to open the door, which nearly hit her in the face as Tibby pushed against the wood.

Minerva stepped back as the door opened with a whoosh. "Is something the matter?"

Tibby's eyes fell to Minerva's upturned, blistered palm. "How in the blazes did that occur?" It was apparently a rhetorical question, because she shook her head and said, "Don't answer." Jack's sister grabbed Minerva by the elbow and led her to the washstand over in the corner. Methodically Tibby lit a candle and then brought Minerva's hand closer to the flame and examined her palm. "Did ye already clean it?"

"I did. Gregory said it's imperative to keep a wound clean, or else sepsis is likely to set in. I don't have any honey, or else I'd have applied some."

"Hmm… Does your brother Gregory always favor natural cures?"

"He's an avid learner in all methods of healing. I should introduce you to him."

"No offense, me lady, but I'd rather you not." Tibby reached into the satchel that hung across her chest and rested against her hip. With swift movements, she rifled through her bag, reading labels until she found a small bottle that she promptly placed between her teeth. Next came a small mixing pot, which she poured water into. After popping the cork from the bottle, Tibby emptied what appeared to be a powder into the bowl and mixed it with her fingers until it turned into a slurry. Scooping up the mixture with her forefinger, Tibby applied it first to the deepest burns and then methodically out from there.

The healer held Minerva's hand over the bowl and rinsed away the paste rather than covering it with a bandage. "Why—" Minerva paused mid-query as a pain radiated up her arm. The burn was deeper than she'd originally believed.

"I don't need more bleedin' lords following me about. Me clients are already nervous as is."

Tibby was still discussing Gregory while Minerva was more curious as to why she had applied the white paste only to wash it off immediately. A bell of warning rang in her mind. "What do you mean, 'more'? How many gentlemen are following you?"

"Hmm…let's see… There was Lord Drake, who followed me about most of the day yesterday, and then early this morn Lord Camdon began following me for a spell before I lost him in King's Square. Mind you, Lord Camdon was the best disguised, but Lord Drake was the hardest to lose." Tibby cleaned out her mixing bowl, dried it with a linen cloth, and tucked it back in her bag.

She turned to face Minerva once more. "And then there was yer brother, Lord Kent, who was trailing behind me for an hour or two this afternoon, after he caught me leaving Malbury Town-house."

"Did Jack send for you?"

"No. I merely went to see me brother to discuss somethin'." She dug into her satchel and withdrew a little jar of honey. "It's no wonder why yer wishing to be Madame Rose. Tenacious hounds, those gentlemen are."

Minerva let out a giggle at Tibby's description of the men. Her smile faded as she confessed, "I'm not certain I wish to be Madame Rose any longer. I'm not as self-sufficient as I thought." She winced as Tibby applied a thin layer of honey and wrapped her hand with a clean strip of cloth. Minerva waved her bandaged hand up in the air. "I've made a terrible mistake."

"Yer hand will heal; no permanent damage."

"I wasn't talking about my hand, Tibby." Minerva sighed.

Tibby frowned as she tucked the supplies back into her bag. "Then wot were you goin' on about?"

Minerva hadn't known Tibby for long, but Jack's sister was steadfast, and Minerva instinctively trusted her. Confiding in a stranger might be soothing. "After you left, Lord Drake appeared at my door last night."

"Well, ain't he clever. And?" Tibby's brows sloped down in the middle to form a deep valley just above her nose.

"He's attracted to Madame Rose in a way he never will be to his best friend's little sister."

"Lady Minerva, yer talkin' to me in riddles. Tell me plain-like."

"Lord Drake only kisses me when I'm Madame Rose. Not when I'm Lady Minerva."

"Yer not making sense. Yer one and the same, me lady." Tibby raised the back of her hand to Minerva's forehead. "Yer not fevered." Hands back on her hips, she continued, "If Lord Drake was smart enough to figure yer location, he's not likely to be confused about who he's kissin'."

"I'm not certain you are correct, but you were right about me. I've come to the realization that I don't really want to be Madame Rose." Minerva sank down on the settee. "I actually prefer my life as Lady Minerva with the option of being Madame Rose…for one night…on the rare occasion."

Tibby sat on the floor then lifted Minerva's skirts and peered and prodded at her knees. "If yer in love with Lord Drake, why not simply lose your match and marry the man?" Apparently satisfied with how the knees were healing, Tibby let go of the skirts.

"It's not that simple."

"Blimey, why do ye peers make things so difficult for yerselves?"

"That's a very good question. One I don't have an answer for."

Tibby shook her head. "Wot are ye afraid of? I'm assuming Lord Drake has already declared himself. Why not marry the man?"

Minerva explained, "Because he'll be marrying Lady Minerva, not Madame Rose."

Tibby kneeled, cupped Minerva's face with both hands, and stared directly into her eyes. "Madness sometimes comes with brilliance, but yer not soft in the head, yer simply confused." She released Minerva and stood, hands on her hips. "'Tis time ye return home."

Minerva smiled. "Only if you accompany me and meet my brother, Gregory."

"Ye need to be focusing on yerself, not trying to play matchmaker." Tibby turned Minerva around by the shoulders. "But since Jack already told me ye never deviate from a plan, I'll go with you before ye badger me more."

"Grand. Let me pack up and we can be off."

"'Tis late. Leave yer things 'ere and I'll bring them to ye tomorrow."

With her injured hand, Minerva wouldn't be able to carry much anyway. She held in a breath, letting the pang of regret subside. Letting go of Madame Rose was harder than she'd thought.

Carefully donning her cloak, Minerva scanned the room one last time. It was the right decision, but in a day's time she would be forced to make a decision—win and remain Lady Minerva Malbury, a spinster for the remainder of her life, or do as Tibby suggested: forfeit the game, become the next Countess of Drake, and marry a gentleman who wished she was someone else. Neither were ideal.

CHAPTER TWENTY-TWO

Anthony entered the Malbury gardens through the service alley. He paused at the sight of rows upon rows of chairs flanking Minerva's favorite chess set on the terrace beneath a mammoth awning. Bloody hell, how many members of the *ton* had Kent invited? His best friend had promised invitations were to be restricted to family and close friends.

He mounted the stairs to the terrace and spied his host, Kent, who stood by the glass double doors.

As Anthony approached, Kent growled, "You are late."

Anthony pulled out his pocket watch. "Actually, I'm exactly on time." He scanned the crowd for his opponent. "Where is Minerva?"

"Inside. Avondale and his cronies are entertaining her and Isadora with stories of adventure and espionage." Kent stepped in front of him, preventing him from finding Minerva. "A quick word."

Anthony hated the idea that Minerva might be charmed by one of the gentleman agents from the Foreign Office. He snapped, "Make it quick."

"Promise me you will succeed where Camdon failed."

Instead of giving his best friend his word, he asked, "You ask this of me, even knowing I might place your sister's life in danger?"

Kent frowned. "Under proper care, fatality rates from child-birth are extremely low. Plus you and I are nothing like our fathers, so it stands to reason our lives should be nothing like that of our sires."

Phyllis joined them and looped her arm through Kent's. "Drake, you must win today. I hate to fathom the schemes that the Head of the Foreign Office might consider implementing should you lose."

"We've both rejected numerous offers from the Head of the Foreign office, and I'd expect Minerva would continue to decline, as I plan to do, even in the event she is to win today," Anthony said.

He attempted to sidestep around the couple, but they shifted in unison, and Kent said, "I want your word on the matter."

Until he could speak to Minerva in private and determine what future she truly desired, Anthony couldn't give Kent his word. "You both know it's no easy feat to defeat Minerva at chess."

Phyllis glanced over her shoulder and then returned her attention to Anthony. "True. But I suspect if anyone could win Minerva's hand in marriage, it would be you."

"My thanks for the vote of confidence." He smiled at Phyllis and avoided Kent's glare.

Kent grumbled, "If you won't give me your word, then at least put my mind at ease by confirming you are playing to win, are you not?"

"I love your sister, and I intend to play with the best of intentions."

"Bah, you are worse than Minerva," Kent complained, and then added, "Stay here. I'll go fetch my sister."

When Kent was out of earshot, Phyllis said, "If you love her, you should fight for her. Play to win."

"I do love her, but I won't force Minerva into marriage, especially not with my family history."

"Don't be a fool, Drake. She loves you." Phyllis laid a hand on his arm and squeezed. "Prove to her you are deserving of her love. After all, she's waited all these years for you."

Guests began to file through the doors and jostle him out onto the terrace. He lost sight of both Phyllis and Kent. He moved along with the flow of guests until he found himself standing next to the chess set.

Guests filled the seats. Anthony's breath caught in his chest as Minerva came into sight, heavily guarded by her siblings, Gregory, Diana, and Isadora. Chestwick and Avondale had Mansville in hand, flanking the man and steering him to a seat between them.

In what seemed like an eternity for Minerva to make her way through the crowd, Anthony stood frozen until she appeared before him.

She dipped into a low curtsy. "Lord Drake." The formal greeting was peculiar.

Reciprocating with a bow, Anthony said, "Lady Minerva. May I have a word before we begin?"

Minerva gave a slight shake of her head, denying him his request. She turned to face Gregory. "Will you do the honor of assisting us in determining who shall go first?"

Her brother smiled, picked up one light pawn and one dark, and placed his hands behind his back. Gregory turned to his sister. "Ladies first."

Minerva pointed to Gregory's left arm, and her brother brought it in front to reveal the light-colored wood piece. Minerva would go first. Anthony was prepared for this. He had multiple strategies devised that would ensure his success, though all but one hinged upon Minerva making a mistake, which the woman rarely did in a game of chess. He wasn't one to depend upon luck, and neither was she.

He pulled out the chair for Minerva and waited for her to slide past him. Mere inches away, he whispered, "Nod if you are playing to win."

Minerva took her seat without acknowledging him.

Anthony rounded the board to slide into his seat. "Ready?"

Minerva removed her gloves and set them in her lap. "I need a moment."

Was she still undecided?

While he waited, he seized the moment to admire her. Minerva was beautiful. Sunshine glinted off her blonde hair and kissed her slightly flushed pink cheeks. He was admiring the next Countess of Drake, but when he blinked, the image of a sated Madame Rose flashed before him.

He shifted in his seat, eager to have Minerva back in his bed. She was staring at him with a slight frown.

He said, "Lady Minerva—"

"Yes, Lord Drake, it is I...Lady Minerva." Her cool tone had him on edge.

"Shall we commence?"

"Let's." She stared directly at him and nodded. Then, with a smirk, she said, "Remember, you owe me a secret each time I place you in check."

A wave of panic rolled through him, and he answered, "I haven't forgotten."

"Then I'm ready." Minerva reached for her queen pawn and moved it forward two spaces forward. A safe and classic first move.

He could mirror Minerva's move and play it safe or have faith in his plan to disguise his moves as those of a beginner. He reached for his rook pawn and moved it a single space forward.

The corner of Minerva's lips twitched. His scheme was working, but how many moves would it take before his opponent became suspicious?

Five. After five moves, he had placed her knight in danger.

She sat back and glanced about the crowd that, for the most part, had lost interest in the game. Even Mansville had lost interest with their rather mundane play. Only a few, which included Kent, Avondale, Diana, and Gregory, continued to pay close attention.

Minerva returned her gaze to his. "Your time with Camdon and Kent was well spent. You don't play like a novice." She picked up her queen and twirled it between her fingers before placing it back on the board in a defensive position to protect her knight.

"Was that a compliment?" He stared at the board. If he continued to remain neutral and not the aggressor, he'd test her patience.

It took six more moves before Minerva hastened the pace of play by kingside castling, shifting her rook toward the center of the board. This was exactly what Anthony had hoped she'd do. Now all he had to do was position his rooks one behind another along the far column to entrap her king. He moved his queen as a sacrifice, copying Minerva's surprise move during her game with Camdon.

Minerva took his queen and asked, "Confident that you can win without the aid of your queen?"

"Mayhap I made an error." He attempted to appear contrite and then promptly took her queen with his pawn. Now neither of them had their queen on the board. They were evenly matched in pieces, although Minerva retained the slight advantage.

"An error?" Minerva picked up her knight and tapped the piece to her chin. "Do you feel remorse for this mistake?"

He was wise enough to know she was not referring to his chess play. "Aye. I'm deeply sorry."

She placed her knight upon the board and sat back to cross her arms over her chest. His attention was momentarily distracted by memories of cupping the delightful breasts that were now trapped beneath her gown.

Minerva searched his features, which he carefully arranged to mask his delight at the progress of the game—and his wayward thoughts. He would have to let her place him in check at least once in order for his plan to win to succeed. Giving up one secret for a lifetime with her as her husband was well worth the price.

He moved his knight into position and waited.

Without hesitation, Minerva moved her knight, placing him in check. "I believe I'm owed a secret, my lord."

"What is it you wish to know?"

Minerva lowered her gaze to the chess pieces. "If you could marry Madame Rose without censure, would you?"

"What in damnation do you mean?" His response slipped through his lips without thought.

She lowered her voice for only him to hear. "You are attracted to Madame Rose, not me as Lady Minerva."

Anthony moved his king one space to his left, easily escaping the threat. "I want to marry you, and it is you who I want to wake up next to every morn."

Minerva continued to avoid his gaze and focused on the board. "Are you certain?"

"Minerva, look at me."

She did as he asked, and lifted a gaze that was filled with fear and confusion.

"If you will have me, it would be an honor to be your husband."

It was her turn, but she didn't reach for any of the pieces.

Minutes later, Kent's form cast a shadow over the board. "Might I suggest a short respite?"

Minerva shook her head. "No. I wish to continue."

Anthony didn't want to rush her. Minerva's next move would tell him whether or not she was truly playing to win or if she was willing to become the Countess of Drake. He held his breath as he waited for her to make her move.

Finally, Minerva reached for her knight and took his knight, again placing them on fairly even footing. It appeared she was still undecided.

Three more turns each, and neither had made moves to end the game quickly. It was time for him to execute his plan. He moved his rook from the far right corner to the far left.

Minerva's brows rose. She acknowledged he was now on the attack.

How would she respond?

She moved her knight to protect her king and counter an attack from his rook. She wasn't ready to lose, but would she mount a counterattack?

"Minerva, do you love me?"

"You have not placed me in check. Why should I answer?"

"Because I need to know before I make my next move."

"Yes. I love you no matter how much I try not to."

Anthony smiled. He would make it his mission to make her happy and to feel loved. He picked up his rook and took her pawn, placing him one step closer to his goal.

Minerva frowned at the board and moved a pawn forward, neither an offensive nor a defensive move.

Drake looked closer at the board. Three more moves and he'd be the winner. Attempting not to appear too eager, he moved his bishop into place. As he expected, Minerva moved her rook to protect her pawn and make room for her king to escape.

He flicked a glance to Kent, who was deep in conversation with his wife. He wanted Kent's blessing one more time, but the man was distracted.

"I see you have finally decided to be the aggressor," Minerva said.

"Does it suit?" He moved his king, which was simply to distract Minerva back to the pieces at the top of the board and away from *her* king.

Minerva moved her bishop into place, on the defense, just as he had hoped. "I'm not certain. Although I will admit that I am enjoying your pursuit."

He assigned their conversation as the reason why Minerva had fallen into his trap. By sacrificing his bishop, he had entrapped her.

As soon as Minerva moved her knight and had captured his bishop, she saw her mistake.

He gave her one more out. "No one is paying any attention to us. Shall we declare a stalemate?"

Minerva surveyed the guests with a quick glance. "Not a chance." With a slight shake of the head and a frown, she studied the board and said, "I can't believe… How did… Where did I…" She blinked with each pause as if reassessing each of her most recent moves. Minerva sat back and with bright, clear eyes, said, "You win."

"Is it that incredible?"

She shrugged. "Do you really wish to marry me?"

"Yes, of course I want to marry you." Why was she stubbornly refusing to accept his suit? "I don't understand your lack of faith in me… Why is it that you do not believe I love you, that I need you, that I desire you and only you?"

Minerva picked up his discarded queen and twirled it between her fingers. "It's not me that you fantasize about at night, is it? It's Madame Rose, isn't it?"

"No." He leaned forward and pleaded with his eyes for her to look at him. "I shouldn't have left you alone the other day. I should have stayed and convinced you to marry me then." He waited for her to raise her hazel eyes from the fallen chess pieces. Once she did, he continued, "I know all too well how facts can become muddled if one is left with only their own thoughts for too long. You are not accustomed to solitary life. I promise you, it is you whom I dream about day and night. I'm not lying when I tell you I want you. I love you."

Her shoulders remained tense. She still didn't believe him, but rather than giving up, Anthony pushed on.

"I admit, two years ago I was enraptured by the attentions of Madame Rose. I won't deny I wanted to bed you then, but perhaps on some level, I knew—I knew you and Madame Rose were one and the same. I let my fears of disappointing Kent and the possibility of killing you prevent me from showing you how I truly felt about you for too long. But I came here today to win your hand, because I love you, and have done so for years. I promise, I desire no one but you, Lady Minerva Malbury. Will you please agree to do me the honor of becoming my wife?"

Minerva discarded the queen she'd been toying with and sat back in her chair. There was a mischievous twinkle in her eyes. "What if Madame Rose wished to make the occasional appearance?" She tilted her head and wrapped a stray curl about her finger.

He pictured waking up next to those silky blonde tresses every morn. A flare of desire replaced the mischievous twinkle in Minerva's gaze. The minx was fully aware he'd grant her whatever it was she wished in return for her promise to marry him.

"I would not be opposed to attending a performance by the mysterious Madame Rose, should she deign to make an appearance."

"And would you be disappointed if she were to retire?"

"The choice is entirely hers." He inched closer to whisper, "Marry me, Minerva."

Extending her arm, she placed her finger on the top of her king and slowly tipped it over. "Anthony Joseph Edmund MacMillian, you win."

"I want to hear you say it, pet."

She leaned forward over the chessboard. "I, Lady Minerva Malbury, agree to marry you."

Not giving a care to who was about, Anthony gave in to temptation, threaded his fingers through her hair, and kissed her soundly, to prove it was she whom he couldn't keep his hands off.

CHAPTER TWENTY-THREE

A COLLECTIVE GASP came from the crowd. She pulled back from Anthony's deep, drugging kiss. Smiling, she turned to search for her sisters, and caught Lord Mansville marching directly toward them. She stiffened in her seat at the sight of the man's scowl and clenched jaw.

Lord Mansville ignored both Anthony and her and stood in front of the board to study the remaining pieces and those discarded to the side. Drake stood prepared to act but remained silent. Meanwhile, every muscle in her back was strung tight, forcing her to sit up straight in her chair. Braced and prepared for the verbal lashing that was sure to come, Minerva held her breath.

Lord Mansville turned on his heel and bestowed upon her what appeared to be a solemn, heartfelt bow. "Lady Minerva, a game well played."

Minerva blinked and narrowed her gaze upon the man she'd feared for three Seasons. "My thanks, Lord Mansville."

"If Lord Drake would be amicable, I'd be honored if you, my lady, would grant me the pleasure of playing another game of chess. I find your style of play extremely fascinating." The man's attention wasn't trained upon her; he was once again studying the board and the pieces. Lord Mansville's obsession wasn't with her, it was with chess and good gameplay.

Minerva studied the man a moment longer with a new perspective. Immersed in the game, the man was blind to the reactions of others, just as she had been.

Drake cleared his throat. "If Lady Minerva wishes to accept your offer to partake in a friendly game of chess, it shall have to wait until after we return from our wedding trip."

Lord Mansville turned to face her future husband, his reluctance to remove his attention from the board obvious. "I shall eagerly await the Countess of Drake's response."

Being referred to as the Countess of Drake even before they were wed had Minerva's pulse racing. For years she had fantasized of holding the title, of being Anthony's wife, and to have her dream come true was truly exciting.

Anthony stepped around the table to join her. "I believe I misread Mansville's intentions entirely."

"I as well." Minerva's lips curved into a smile, and Anthony mirrored the action. The man was incredibly handsome in her opinion and made her heart flutter every time he smiled at her. She swallowed her contented sigh and said, "Are you ready? My family are about to descend upon us."

"I am, but are you?"

Minerva frowned. "Why would I not be?"

"They will have questions." Anthony waggled her brows at her. "Are you prepared?"

"You won, fair and square."

"Their inquisition won't be over the validity of the game. None of them care about chess. They only care about you and your welfare."

"Then they should all be delighted to know I am happy."

"Are you?" Anthony took her hands in his.

"Of course."

His brow creased. "I do not deserve you."

"What are you two whispering about?" Diana wedged her way between them. "I insist on the two of you maintaining the socially acceptable distance between you."

Minerva scowled at having her baby sister play chaperone. "We are to wed, Diana."

Diana asked Anthony, "Do you have a special license to be wed?"

To Minerva's surprise, Anthony placed a hand over his jacket and patted his chest. "In fact, I do—however, I need a few moments alone with your sister before we send for Reverend Brown."

Chestwick arched a brow in Minerva's direction, and when she nodded, her brother-in-law came to their rescue. "I'm sure Diana and I can arrange for a diversion."

"But love," Diana replied.

"Minerva assisted me, and I shall return the favor." Chestwick took his wife's hand and looped it through his arm. "I shall distract Kent, Phyllis, and Gregory. Can you handle Avondale, Isadora, and Charlotte?"

"As you wish, husband." Diana gave Minerva a narrowed stare over her shoulder and said, "Ten minutes, not a moment longer."

"When did she become the overprotective one?" Anthony asked.

"I think it's an early onset of maternal instinct," Minerva replied.

His brow shot up. "Diana is pregnant already?"

"Why are you surprised?"

"Our family is growing exponentially."

Anthony's use of *our* made her heart flip. She had made the right choice. "Aye, and it's wonderful."

Anthony escorted her back into the house. He nodded and smiled as guests congratulated him as they strode through the terrace doors, through the drawing room, and made their way to the family parlor that Minerva favored.

Ensconced in the private haven, Minerva's muscles relaxed.

As soon as the latch fell into place, Anthony gathered her in his arms. "I have a confession to make."

She stiffened in his arms, bracing herself for the worst. He'd changed his mind. He didn't want to marry her after all.

He placed a kiss upon her forehead. "I purposely forfeited the chess match we played all those years ago, to make you smile. I won today's match to do the same. Can you forgive me for not challenging you sooner…for not asking you to marry me, when it was all my heart desired?"

"I shan't forgive you, for there is nothing to forgive. While I'll admit the last several years have been a challenge, they also brought to light what I am capable of and made me realize what exactly it is that I want."

"We don't have to marry by special license if you do not wish to. But the archbishop was kind enough to grant me an audience, and—"

"Yes. I think you've made me wait long enough. And everyone who I'd want present is on the other side of those doors."

Anthony chuckled. "No doubt attempting to eavesdrop." He bent and kissed her. "Let's get married."

EPILOGUE

T HE INFANT CRADLED in his arm stole Anthony's heart. He had been born a healthy eight pounds, nineteen inches, and with a pair of lungs that rivaled an opera singer's.

Anthony glanced across the chessboard at the babe's mother, his hale wife, who was presently scowling at the pieces in front of her. It was her turn to make a move, and after enduring nine months of his incessant queries as to her health and worrying over every aspect of her pregnancy, Minerva deserved a little patience from him.

His son wiggled and yawned before promptly closing his eyes to slumber. Anthony acknowledged all his worrying had been for naught. Minerva gave birth to their first child without issue, and had given him her "I told you not to worry" look thereafter.

A small hand tugged at his elbow. "Uncle, uncle… I want to see the babe." Julian, their eldest nephew at the age of five, who had been Anthony's boon companion during Minerva's pregnancy, peered down at his cousin. "Have you decided upon a name for him yet?"

Minerva mumbled, "Not yet. Do you have any suggestions?"

Anthony hadn't imagined ever having a son, and thus naming his firstborn had resulted in endless discussions with his wife, all with Minerva stating she knew a "so and so" and she'd not have her child share the same name.

"I think..." Julian's brows knitted as he concentrated. "Emmett."

Diana waddled over and swooped in and picked up her son. "It's not your place to name the babe. That's the parents' responsibility."

"Emmett is a good name, Mama." Julian had inherited his papa's looks and his mama's stubbornness.

Diana shrugged and Julian grinned at Anthony, displaying the devilish dimple that would get the boy into trouble and out of it all too many times as he matured.

Arms reached out for their child, Minerva said, "I believe Julian has a point. Emmett is a fine name. However..." Anthony handed over his son to Minerva, who peered down at the sleeping baby. "He looks to me more like a Gavin to me—Gavin Emmett MacMillian."

Anthony refrained from mentioning that a quarter of his clansmen up north were named Gavin.

"I like it, Auntie M." Julian wiggled from his mama's arms and jumped up to snuggle next to Minerva. The young boy glanced at the chessboard and then tugged at her skirts. Minerva bent lower so Julian could whisper into her ear.

Minerva reached for her bishop's pawn and moved it forward one space, effectively blocking Anthony from taking her queen. The lad had picked up the game quickly—not surprising, since his father, Chestwick, was a skilled strategist himself, even if he didn't share a love for the game.

The patter of more small feet approaching had Anthony ignoring the chess match and slipping down to his knees from his seat, crouched down and ready for the onslaught of hugs from Kent's little ones—Harris, who was now four, and Sophie, fourteen months younger but more than capable of keeping up with her rambunctious brother and older cousin Julian.

Kent's children were inseparable, and they ran toward him in unison. Arms spread wide at the ready, Anthony braced for impact.

The pair yelled, "Uncle, uncle… Where is the babe?"

Anthony hugged the mites tight and picked them up, one in each arm. "Come meet your cousin Gavin."

A bedraggled Kent and Phyllis entered the drawing room. Kent headed directly to the sideboard, while Phyllis placed a hand on each of her children's shoulders to settle them.

Phyllis gave Minerva a smile. "My, you look well." She reached for her nephew, and Minerva handed little Gavin over.

Harris turned and pleaded, "Mama, we want to see Gavin."

Phyllis walked over to the settee and sank down in the middle, and was quickly surrounded by all the children in the room. Gavin would soon join their ranks running about the estate, but until then, Anthony would heed Kent and Chestwick's advice to enjoy every moment the babe was stationary.

Minerva flicked her gaze to the empty seat opposite her. She was eager to play.

They hadn't played against each other since he'd won her hand. The terms had been set earlier at breakfast. The winner would be granted the first move in their private chambers for a week. Bed sport with Minerva was the best alternative to chess. Anthony no longer played out chess moves in his head—now he fantasized about how to please his wife each and every day and night.

Minerva beamed at him and stole his heart once more.

He studied the board and the pieces in front of him. It had taken three years and the healthy births of his nephews and niece before Anthony gained the courage to attempt having a family. With Gavin in their lives, he wasn't about to wait another three years to try for another child.

The giggles from the children and the oohs and ahhs from his sisters-in-law filled his heart and furthered his resolve to win today's chess match.

With the room filled with family, Anthony sent up a thank you to the heavens for blessing him with the most patient and understanding wife, and then prayed for the wisdom to defeat his wife and begin the process of adding to their family. Duart Hall was going to be filled with love and little MacMillians, all because Minerva never settled for anything less than love.

About the Author

Rachel Ann Smith writes steamy historical romances with a twist. Her debut series, Agents of the Home Office, features female protagonists that defy convention.

When Rachel isn't writing, she loves to read and spend time with the family. She is frequently found with her Kindle by the pool during the summer, on the side-lines of the soccer field in the spring and fall or curled up on the couch during the winter months.

She currently lives in Colorado with her extremely understanding husband and their two very supportive children.

Visit Rachel's website for updates on cover reveals and new releases – www.rachelannsmith.com.

You can also stay up to date with Rachel following her on social media.

Facebook: rachelannsmit11
BookBub: bookbub.com/authors/rachel-ann-smith
Amazon: amazon.com/Rachel-Ann-Smith/e/B07THSRH6B
Twitter: @rachelannsmit11
Instagram: instagram.com/rachelannsmithauthor
Goodreads:
goodreads.com/author/show/19301975.Rachel_Ann_Smith